MW01129641

GASLIGHT
PARADISE

GASLIGHT
PARADISE

by
Walrus

GASLIGHT PARADISE © 2019

All rights reserved. No part of this book may
be reproduced in any form or by any electronic or
mechanical means, including information storage
and retrieval systems, without written permission
from the author, except in the case of a reviewer,
who may quote briefpassages embodied in critical
articles or in a review.

This is a work of fiction. Names, characters,
places, and incidents either are the product of the
author's imagination or are used fictitiously, and
any resemblance to actual persons, living or dead,
events, or locales is entirely coincidental.

Typeset version: 2

ISBN: 9781698863078

Cheers. To us.

Prologue

A ring of eight, black-robed people chanted in a circle around the tiny, hooded figure that was laid out on the heavy marble altar. Their voices were muffled beneath the pointed hoods they wore over their faces, but their eyes glinted through slits in the fabric.

The poor figure on the altar was covered with a thick black hood that had no holes for breathing or sight. Dark-red velvet spilled from beneath the fragile form and down the altar's sides in crimson waves.

The group was led by a tall figure at the head of the circle holding a large ancient tome as they performed their ritual in the old, private library where the altar was placed. Their voices were muted by rows of books lining the bookshelves that covered the walls up to the high ceiling. A row of enormous floor-to-ceiling windows draped with black velvet curtains lined the back wall. Flames flickered in the candlesticks around the room, jumping fitfully with the rise of their voices.

The circle's menacing chanting increased in intensity, and a dark, otherworldly roar built slowly along with them. The deep roar escalated in a wave of sound and fury until it hurt the chanters' ears; then suddenly, the leader of the ceremony snapped the ancient book shut with authority.

Everything became silent.

The dimly lit library was still.

The candles guttered in their stands, almost going out.

Through the old walls came the very slightest reverberation, the well-muffled sounds of the raging party down the hall. But they seemed distant and inconsequential.

The ink-black shadows painting the room deepened, hinting at some vast, unknowable thing that lurked beyond. A feeling floated in the air, barely tangible – like some inexorable force was being set in motion, some vast and ancient thing reaching across from the beyond to touch this world.

The air was electric.

The leader set the large book aside and slowly drew a long-bladed knife, about a hand's width and the length of a forearm, that gleamed in the light from the candles. Without a word, the rest of the figures pulled out knives and raised them high.

The blades shimmered in the darkness. The low roar returned, swelling and growing in volume and intensity.

The room—the tiny, robed form on the altar; the

circle of hooded figures with their knives glowing in the dim light; the shadows enveloping them—it all took on a crystalline air. The roar grew until it whipped at their ears, and every molecule in the universe came into extreme focus for one split second.

Then they struck.

The blades all plunged at the same time, down into the tiny black-robed human, cutting through skin and piercing it all at once, like some poor animal, and just like that, as has so often been the case throughout history, a life was coldly, callously ended in hope of personal gain. The roar lifted into a formless, furious crescendo and ended abruptly with the last heartbeat of the tiny figure's life.

A second passed.

The air was still. The rushing noise had stopped, but something remained: an ancient power. Though the world seemed like it had just come to an end inside the confines of the old, thick walls, all the figures in the circle could once again dimly hear the murmur of the people outside the walls.

An uncomfortable moment passed.

Then abruptly, the tiny figure on the altar sat up.

The hooded figures gasped.

The tiny form, still bleeding into the black robe, silently pointed at something behind them all.

Slowly, they followed the finger with their eyes.

Part One

Break from Reality

Pfenigton, Maine.

A little slice of forgotten Americana nestled in the thick, old trees that lined the coast. It had been founded a long time ago for some reason or other, but no one could quite remember why. All anyone knew was it was located in a remote area in Maine for seemingly no reason whatsoever, and the town was and always had been off by itself in its own little world.

Mostly because no one much wanted to live there. Or anywhere near there.

With his dark-brown eyes reflecting the white light of the morning mist, Darnell glanced over his shoulder at the Randy Beaver, the local watering hole, as he crossed the street. The supple soles of his black leather Italian loafers scuffed on the rough asphalt as he walked toward Pop's Diner, a greasy spoon affair in the center of the sleepy one-light town.

He had a face with the innocent but worn look of a man who'd made it into middle age with a degree of lingering naivete. He fiddled with the top black button on the jacket of his two-piece navy-blue suit as he stepped up from the street onto the sidewalk in front of Pop's Diner.

He was due to meet his old friend Rod around noon and had no idea what to expect. All he knew was what Rod had told him in a phone call three days earlier.

"I'm being escorted out of the studio," Rod's voice said over the phone, sounding quite manic. "There's been drama on set. They've cancelled my show."

He'd sounded absolutely heartbroken.

"That's awful," Darnell had told him. "I can barely hear you. Why is the connection so bad?"

"Dude. I'm calling from the gas station next to the studio. This awesome guy behind the counter let me borrow his phone. Thanks again, guy."

When Rod phoned Darnell, he was still dressed in the dark-blue, pinstriped suit of his lawyer character Arturo Ricardo from TV as he nodded to the gas station clerk. His thin black tie was crumpled and his white button-up stained with sweat. His dirty-blond hair was slicked down, one stray curl loose at the front, and his fake debonair mustache was firmly askew.

The clerk smiled sarcastically, looking sweaty and

high. "No problem 'Arturo.' Just don't prosecute me."

Rod's face could be seen on the TV behind the counter. His newly cancelled TV show was playing in the background.

"It's Rod, thanks," Rod said to the clerk.

"I know, man. You called me," Darnell said.

"What? Never mind, it doesn't matter. The bastards took my company phone."

"Sounds like your day's been terrible," Darnell said, checking his watch.

"It has been!"

"It's not even noon yet," Darnell said, munching on a loaded baked potato with no bacon.

"You're telling me! I can't handle all this shit right now. I need help," Rod said.

"Rod, man, what kind of drama could have possibly made them cancel your show?" Darnell had asked.

"Something … baaad. Look. I need to get out of L.A. for a while."

"Well, I'm on assignment this next week," Darnell had said, "the firm is sending me to bumblefuck nowhere coastal Maine. You're more than welcome to come along. It might do you good."

"Dude, that sounds like just what I need. Just give me a day to put the word out around L.A., that I've arranged a little getaway. To account for my disappearance. I can't let it look like weakness. These jackals all smell blood."

"Okay," Darnell had said. "Are you ever going to tell me what's going on?"

"When we meet. Not over the phone. Besides, I

need to ask you something."

©

Standing in front of Pop's Diner, Darnell ran his hand over his shaved bald head and peeked at his watch.

11:51 a.m.

He pushed through the entrance, and a tiny brass bell at the top of the door tinkled to announce his arrival. His shaven face warmed as he entered the diner and came in from the cool air.

A skeletal man with thinning black hair in a black wool trench coat sitting at the far booth looked up from his newspaper. The man's startlingly pigmentless eyes peered over the top of his paper.

Darnell looked away from the man and smiled when he saw his old friend sitting a few booths up.

Rod sat hunched forward in a booth, cradling his dirty-blond-haired head in his hands. His classically chiseled features were looking a little wan, but his cheeks were the flushed red of an alcoholic. He kept his sunglasses in place over his deep blue eyes even inside the diner, trying unsuccessfully to hide his discomposure.

The inside of the diner was your typical middle-of-nowhere place. Cracked linoleum on the floor and crumbling tiles in the ceiling. The bar was the centerpiece, lined with round, red, vinyl-topped stools with a view of the kitchen. A portly cook was busy making an order of hash browns and scrapple for a couple at the bar. An old CRT TV with bent rabbit-ear antennae ran some standard-fare morning show in the background. The tinny audio crackled from the old paper cone speaker.

The beautiful plastic hosts of the morning television show babbled happily in the background.

"Long night?" Darnell asked Rod in a friendly tone, as if they'd hung out only yesterday. He leaned over to clap his old friend on the shoulder and sat down on the Formica bench across from him.

The dark aviator sunglasses Rod wore hid the visible signs of what can only be described as one enormous, lifelong bender. Rod removed his dark shades and revealed red, bloodshot eyes.

"All my nights are long," Rod croaked.

"You're not used to staying up late by now?" Darnell rolled his eyes.

"Ugh," Rod said. "Won't you let me die in peace."

The cheerful waitress ambled to the table.

"Morning, fellas. Can I take your order?" She pulled out a little paper pad and a pen.

"Two coffees, please," Darnell said.

"Lots of cream and sugar," Rod said in a raspy voice, not looking at her.

Darnell smiled at the waitress, and she smiled back.

"I'll be back in a jiff," she said happily and walked back to the kitchen.

"Wish I could drink like I was twenty," Rod said. "But I can't anymore."

"Neither can I," Darnell said. "We're not twenty anymore, in case you hadn't noticed."

"I've been trying not to," Rod said.

Darnell laughed.

"So what happened?" Darnell asked.

"I'll explain it all after we get something to eat," Rod replied absently.

"Seriously?"

"Aren't you just happy to see your old friend?" Rod asked as he looked at Darnell.

After a moment of contemplation, a wide smile appeared on Darnell's face. "I honestly am. We haven't seen each other in years.

Rod pinched the bridge of his nose.

"I'm going to die if I don't eat soon," he said. "This hangover is a monster."

"Let's feed that beast," Darnell chuckled.

He picked up a little tabletop ad for the daily specials. On the glossy cardboard was a close-up shot of perfectly buttered stacks of flapjacks.

"BOTTOMLESS PANCAKES SERVED TILL NOON, DAILY," the ad stated.

"This beast could use about a pound of bacon," Rod stated gravely.

Darnell glanced at the old clock on the wall.

11:58 a.m.

"Don't worry, dude. We'll get you some. Just don't expect me to eat any," he said.

The waitress walked up with two porcelain cups of piping hot coffee and set them down in front of Rod and Darnell.

"Ma'am," Darnell said, "can we still get those bottomless pancakes from your ad here?"

She checked the clock on the wall, and gave him a sly look over her large frame glasses. "Just in time, huh? Okay."

"Thank you," Darnell smiled. "Pancakes and lots of syrup then, please."

"And extra bacon," Rod added.

She smiled.

"You want anything else, dear?" she asked Rod.

"Just more of that beautiful smile," he rasped, as he came up from slurping his coffee.

"Oh hush. I'll be right back with your order." The waitress softened up at that, and walked off with a little pep in her step.

Rod gazed into his coffee, the color slowly creeping into his face.

"You okay, bud?" Darnell asked.

Rod paused before answering. "Yeah, man. I'm so glad to be away from all those people, with their lattes and their scripts," he said. "I mean, the fact that I'm actually drinking a regular coffee right now is blowing my mind."

Darnell chuckled and nodded.

The waitress walked up with their orders and placed heaps of steaming hot pancakes and crispy bacon on the table. The white porcelain plates clinked on the Formica tabletop.

Rod threw a generous pat of butter on each of his pancakes and proceeded to drown them in syrup.

"Mmmmm," he said, as he chewed the fluffy, buttery pancakes, so hot they were letting off curls of steam.

The waitress turned the TV up as she walked behind the counter, and the hosts' babbling came into clearer focus.

"...re such a minx," Jenny said, tossing her luscious black hair, and giving Jessica a conspiratorial look.

"I'm no minx," Jessica said in a feisty voice. "I'm a jungle cat. A tiger!"

"Rawr girl!" Jenny said. "Let 'em know!"

"*Omigod!* It's so funny you said that," Jamilla burst out.

"What, girl?" Jenny and Jessica both said in near unison before bursting out laughing.

"Did. You. See?" she asked with a serious look on her face, eyelids half lowered, lips pursed.

"What, girl!" they both exclaimed at the same time.

"Rodney Richardson," Jamilla said in a loaded tone. "Can you believe? They cancelled his show!"

"Arturo, nooooo," Jessica cried.

"I knowwwww," Jenny wailed. "He was so beautiful, and now I can't see his gorgeous face cross-examining sexy witnesses on *Law & Lace* anymore!"

"It really is a tragedy," Jessica said. "He's perfect."

"I know!" Jamilla said.

"So what happened, girl?" Jenny asked, leaning in. "Gimme the juicy stuff."

"I don't even know," Jamilla said. "They said he brought his tiger to the set, and it bit an intern or something."

"Oooh, and after all that bad-boy behavior, that's what finally broke the network?" Jessica asked.

"Guess so, girl," Jamilla said. "I. Guess. So."

"I hear *he's* the one who's broke," Jessica said. "All those parties and private jets."

"Giant paintings. White tigers. Drugs and Ferraris," Jamilla nodded. "My second husband was exactly like that. Just spent every damn thing. His therapist said it was a disorder."

"I heard he bought a solid-gold, ancient egyptian sarcophagus with a credit card or something," Jenny said, "for $30 million, and now they're going to auction it off to help pay off his debts."

"Oooh, a Black Card!"

The three hosts kept pressing Jamilla to dish more as the patrons and waitstaff of Pop's Diner started looking back and forth from the television screen to the booth where Rod and Darnell sat.

A man, in khaki shorts and a ventilated fishing shirt, leaned over and whispered something into his wife's ear. She squinched her painted brows in concern and then arched them in amazement.

Darnell looked at Rod with concern.

Rod sighed. "Man, I came here to avoid exactly this kind of shit."

"I don't know what to tell you," Darnell said. "You're super famous."

"More like super fucked," Rod muttered under his breath and wolfed down the rest of his pancakes and bacon. He gulped down his coffee, then tossed his thin paper napkin on the table and stood up. "Pay the nice lady, Darnell. Let's blow this popsicle stand."

Darnell threw a couple of twenties on the table and stood up too.

The gaunt, sharp-eyed man in the black wool

trench coat put his gloved hands on the table and abruptly pushed himself up out of the booth he was sitting in, all the while keeping his pale, pigmentless eyes locked on Rod and Darnell.

"You fellas okay?" the waitress called as she walked out of the kitchen.

The sharp-eyed man began walking purposefully toward them.

"Who the hell is that guy?" Rod muttered.

"I don't know, but he's coming over here."

"Get me out of here," Rod said under his breath, as he made a beeline to the door.

The bell tinkled as they left Pop's Diner.

Darnell looked behind them as the door closed, but the sharp-eyed man was gone.

Outside in the parking lot, a disaffected-looking teenager leaned up against an old sedan, smoking an unfiltered cigarette.

"You two staying up at the cabin near the old property?" he asked.

"Maybe," Rod replied. "Why do you care?"

"Y'all don't wanna mess around out in those woods. Lotta people went missing up there in the 1920s."

"How do you know that?" Darnell asked.

The teenager chuckled, his limp brown hair shaking. He brushed it from his eyes and inhaled from the cigarette again.

"Everybody around here knows it, fella. But I know it cuz my granddaddy was the groundskeeper up there, way back. Showed me all the original newspaper clippings and everything."

"What's that got to do with us?" Rod asked.

"Depends," the boy replied.

"On what?" Darnell asked.

"On how stupid you are," the boy said, and stubbed out his cigarette butt.

Rod clapped Darnell on the shoulder and laughed at his surprised expression.

"Don't let these superstitious hillbillies bother you, Darnell," Rod said. "Let's get the fuck out of here."

At the Vending Machines

Goosebumps ran across Aimee's exposed arms as she walked into the bright, cold vending machine room. Banks of options lined each machine's face in the wall-to-wall row of them that stood lined up in front of her.

Her tight, formal black dress and wave of raven-black hair soaked up the blue light that emanated from the plethora of choices, while her brown eyes, the buckles on her stylish black purse, and her shiny black stiletto heels reflected all of the backlit, colorful logos on the buttons.

After much deliberation, she eventually settled for her usual selection of a chocolate Dingbar and a Tiger Cola.

As she pressed the buttons for her selections, her immaculately manicured fingernails, which were painted a glossy eggshell pink, reflected the light like slick plastic. The drink came out immediately, but the candy bar only moved slowly as the mechanism pitifully whined.

Eventually, the machine ground to a halt, and her candy bar got stuck.

She began to daydream for a moment.

In her daydream, she crouched down and leaned against the machine. She slipped her hand into the dispenser, and reaching up, got her arm all the way in, up to the bicep.

Her hand was almost there.

Her fingers were about to close.

Then, just as she was about to reach it, to her immense surprise, the vending machine clamped down on her arm, and started growling like a monster.

A stern male voice broke her daydream.

"I was hoping you'd be here," said an immaculately dressed old man. "You look quite exquisite in that dress, Aimee, I must say."

He'd walked up behind her while she was standing there daydreaming and snapped her out of her reverie.

Marky's imperious face was craggy, crazed with fine lines and wrinkles, and his eyebrows were thickets of white hair mounted over cloudy, blue eyes. The hair on his head was snow-white but still thick. His finely tailored suit was a deep purple, almost black, with red pinstripes, and his shoes were a beautiful black leather. His frail old body was kept upright mechanically. The million dollar joints on his delicate robotic frame could be heard whirring invisibly beneath his well-tailored suit as he moved, apparently naturally.

"Uh, thanks, I guess," Aimee said. "I'm always here

late, where else would I be?"

Marky looked her up and down in her one piece black dress that hugged close to her body and ended mid thigh. "You work like that?" he asked.

"I was supposed to be at the theater," she said, and folded her arms across her breasts.

"No longer?"

"I'm still trying to make it out in time."

Marky's gaze lingered on her legs as he said, "It's wonderful to see you so dedicated to us. To … your work."

"Okay," Aimee said uncomfortably, giving him a sidelong look, and then back at her stuck candy bar.

"Want me to get that for you?" He asked.

"It's not going to take the CEO, Marky. I can handle it."

"Oh good," Marky said, licking his dry lips with a sandpaper tongue. "I'll stand back and watch. Remember not to lift with your back, dear."

She pressed her shoulder into the face of the stalled machine, put her foot under the bottom, and pushed it onto two legs, rocking it back and dropping it sharply. She unstuck not only her own candybar but another one as well. Marky stood back with a salacious look in his ancient green eyes and an enigmatic smile on his face. She picked up the other bar and offered it to Marky.

"You want this extra Dingbar?" she asked.

"You'll know when I want something," he replied. "Have you made any breakthroughs with the P10?"

"We're getting closer," she said cautiously. "The new study is promising."

"Bring me some good news, Ms. Xiao. There's a lot riding on you." Marky smirked.

She glanced at him sideways. The lights of the vending machines lit their faces and illuminated their eyes.

"When the campus is quiet like this and it's just us and the computers and the lights going, it all feels quite insular," Aimee commented. "Like a little bubble in the night. It seems so fragile."

"I wouldn't worry about it, Aimee," Marky said, moving closer to her, his delicate mechanical frame whirring. "If things are good, no need to question why."

"I'm not going to make any breakthroughs standing here at the vending machines chatting with you," she said, recoiling from him.

"Very true," Marky said, his frame darkening the door to the room as she backed quickly away. "Don't take too long. Some of us aren't so young."

Cabin in the Woods

The cabin Darnell's firm had rented was a little clapboard affair on the northern Atlantic coast of Maine. It was tidily constructed, the sides were covered in worn white paint, and the whole thing was set back off the road, obscured by sugar maples.

Inside the cabin, the cabinets and tables were all made of rough-hewn logs, but the seating and light fixtures were all sleekly architectural, futuristic designs.

"The Atlantic looks like a depressing piece of shit today." Rod squinted into the sun as he looked out the back window. "There's no people. This weather sucks. This is not the beach I signed up for."

The sun had moved lazily through its arc and was more than three-quarters of the way across the sky.

"It's Maine, Rod, what did you expect?" Darnell said, sitting on the angular leather couch, holding a glass of whiskey. "This cabin is nice and cozy, and this weather is basically perfect for Maine. What's the problem?"

"With a liquor cabinet this big, I guess I can deal with anything," Rod said as he walked over to the side of the comfortable living room to the giant bar and liquor cabinet and poured himself a whiskey.

"So what have they got you doing this time? This looks pretty fancy for Maine." Rod gestured around with his drink, indicating the cabin.

"I've got to go out and confirm some survey numbers," Darnell said as he took a sip of his whiskey.

"'Confirm some survey numbers,'" Rod quoted him in a dry tone, "in your five-thousand-dollar Italian shoes? There have to be surveyors for that."

"Apparently, the client had some questions. I honestly didn't realize how remote this place was." He tipped his glass at Rod. "It's good to have you here."

The cabin was quiet for a moment.

When the moment passed, Rod produced a mason jar with a friendly looking label and a cute square tag dangling from a bit of twine wound around the rim.

"What is *that*?"

"A nice man my agent knows gave it to me. It was from one of my production companies as a parting gift," Rod said as he gestured with the jar. "Said it was supposed to 'show me the way,' you know?"

"Some nice production company rep your agent knows says the stuff in that jar with the friendly packaging is supposed to 'show you the way'?" Darnell repeated slowly, gesturing with air quotes.

"I dunno. Why not? I figured I'd give it a try." Rod shrugged. "I mean, it's the whole point of this trip."

"Oh *really?*" Darnell asked in a flat tone, giving his friend a sideways look. "I thought the whole point of this trip was to 'get away'."

"This *will* help us get away," Rod said as he hefted the jar of plant matter and tapped the label with his finger. It had instructions printed on it, explaining how to make tea from the faintly glowing red dust in the jar. "Help me get away from my creditors," Rod joked with a sad smile. "All I know is they took everything I had, and I'm just trying to figure out what to do next."

"What do you mean, they took everything?" Darnell asked seriously.

"They're probably waiting in my condo to break my legs as we speak. Little do they know," Rod said laughing. "I don't own the place anymore."

"That's not funny, Rod," Darnell said.

"I know. Let's just take this, and maybe I can forget about all this shit for a while."

"Is it that bad?" Darnell asked. "That you need to take that shit to escape?"

Rod looked his friend in the eye. "Is that so strange, Darnell?" Rod asked. "Don't you have problems?"

"I dunno." Darnell said. "I mean … life's just been a blur since Memaw died. But I never really think about 'getting away' from it. I just keep plugging away every day like I always do."

"Dude, you gotta let that shit go. Snap out of it,"

Rod said. "Memaw died twenty years ago. You're telling me the last twenty years have been a blur? That's crazy!"

"And taking these drugs are supposed to help with that?"

"Come on, man. Just drink with me for a while. Top us up?" Rod asked, handing his glass to Darnell.

"Fine," Darnell said, downed his drink and walked over to the bar to fill their glasses.

Rod walked over to the kitchen alcove, found a pot, filled it with water, and placed it all on the stovetop. He followed the cutely constructed instructions on the jar.

"How to drink me," the card read. "First boil water and steep one teaspoon per cup of water boiled."

Rod hovered over the stove and added a few liberal teaspoons of the glowing red granules to the water in the pot.

"Dude, calm down," Darnell said, returning with two drinks. "Don't make it too strong."

"Oh, calm down yourself," said Rod, taking his drink from Darnell. "Don't be a weenie."

Darnell rolled his eyes, and drank half of his drink in one swig.

Rod stirred the pot as the water began to boil.

"You ever think about selling that big old house of yours and financing a Hollywood movie?" Rod asked, seemingly out of nowhere.

"What?" Darnell asked, startled.

"What?"

"You must be joking."

"Sure," Rod said, raising his hands in a conciliatory manner. "Of course I was. Look, tea's done."

Darnell finished his drink and took the tea Rod handed him.

The two walked out on the back porch with their teacups and studied the view that stretched out in front of them. The Atlantic reflected pale orange and red from the setting sun in its gray waters, and the sky was large and clear above it.

They watched a satellite whiz by high overhead, a tiny white light screeching silently across space.

"It's nice out here," Rod said, looking around at the scenery.

Darnell nodded.

Waves crashed in the distance, and the sound of the ocean washed through the gaps in their conversation.

"This stuff smells awful," Darnell said uneasily, sniffing his steaming cup of tea. "I wonder what it is?"

"Don't worry so much," Rod said.

They both drank from their teacups and let the salt air whip at their clothes. Eventually, they finished their drinks and set them down on the table.

"I feel restless," Darnell said.

"Me too," Rod said and stood up. "Let's walk up the beach and stretch our legs."

Darnell nodded, and they made their way down the wooden steps that led from the deck to the sand.

Late

Darkness blanketed the balmy summer night. Aimee was breaking into a sweat just sitting with the air conditioner off. She was pressed into the front seat of her small silver car as she rummaged around in her purse, knowing full well there weren't any cigarettes in it but still irrationally hoping that she might find a stray one.

There were none.

She sighed deeply and expanded her search to the straight lines of her car's dashboard and center console, looking everywhere. After searching all over, she finally fished a stale, half-smoked one from between the driver's seat and the armrest.

Opening the car's thin aluminum door to get some cooler air, or at least a slight breeze, she lit the cigarette and inhaled from it.

The tobacco crackled.

The hot asphalt of the parking lot shimmered in

the heat of the night. Angular benches and walk-
ways lined the perimeter of the lot. Streetlights on
poles with spindly aluminum arms arced out over it
all, casting bright orange pools of light, dotting the
sparsely populated rows of parking spaces, and painting Aimee's face orange.

The words "Sequentia Center" reflected on her
windshield – the sign for the office complex where she
worked was lit up overhead like a beacon.

Aimee grabbed her phone from where it lay face
up on the gray simulated leather center console of her
car and called her sister.

The phone rang twice before she picked up.

"Hello?" Her sister's voice sounded trebly.

"Lunette, I'm so glad you picked up," Aimee said.
"I couldn't *not* call you."

"What happened?" Lunette asked, intrigued.

"My boss is such a creep. Just, ew."

"Your boss? I thought he was on vacation."

"Well, not my direct boss. The CEO of Sequentia."

"The actual CEO was gross to you? Ew, what did
he do?"

"My fucking Dingbar got stuck in the vending
machine, and he said he wanted to 'stand back and
watch' while I rocked the machine. Fucking *gross, ugh!*"
She shivered at the memory.

"That's terrible!" Lunette said. "You have to report
it!"

Aimee didn't respond at first.

"I think he's been watching me, Lunette. He
kept asking me about any breakthroughs I might be

making. What the hell does he even know about any breakthroughs I might be on the verge of making? He's like twelve levels above me!"

"You're on the verge of a breakthrough?" Lunette asked.

"I shouldn't have said that. Don't focus on that; focus on how he knows way too much about me and lurks around the soda machines like a creepy old vampire every night I work late."

"He had no right to say that," Lunette said. "You really should report him."

"To who, Lunette? He's the CEO, and he was looking at my girls like they were the fountain of youth," Aimee said. "This dress makes my girls look amazing."

"At least you know you look great in that dress!" Lunette joked.

"Shut up! I have a date tonight," Aimee said. "Can I help it that I like to get fancy on a Friday night every now and then?"

"Well, as long as he didn't pinch your butt or something, I guess," Lunette said.

"No, nothing that far."

"Well, good. I'm glad you're okay. Your CEO sounds like a gross old perv."

Aimee laughed.

"Hey, what time is it?" She glanced at the slim golden watch on her wrist, unable to see its face in the dim orange light of the parking lot.

"Twenty to eight," Lunette replied. There was a sound of glasses clinking in the background. "Weren't you supposed to be out of there, like, an hour ago?"

"Mind your own business, Lunette," Aimee said, laughing.

"Okay, okay," Lunette said, sounding like she was scooping ice from the freezer. "I wasn't trying to pry."

"Yes, you were, but it's mostly harmless," Aimee said. "I was supposed to be out of here an hour ago. But I want to wrap this thing up before I go."

"Everybody gets it, Aimee. You're an overachiever. But don't you have to make it to the theater before the curtains open? I thought they locked the doors once the play starts."

"Ugh, I know." Aimee answered in a withering tone. "It's ridiculous. Who takes a date to the theater anymore?"

As she gesticulated to emphasize her words, her small car rocked slightly.

"You always did have a short attention span," said Lunette in a wry voice.

"Shut up, Lunette," she said, half joking. "I hate blind dates. And I can't stand that Mother had any-thing to do with it."

"Listen, the point is, you work too much," Lunette said. "Take some time off ... for yourself."

"I don't work too much, Lunette." Aimee got out of her car.

"Aimee. C'mon. You're always tired," Lunette said. "What is it you're even working on?"

Aimee wiped the sweat off her lip, closed her flim-sy little car's door with a light clunk, and locked it.

"You know I can't tell you!" Aimee said. "I'm so tired of repeating that to you."

She walked back through the futuristic looking campus of her work toward the lab and smoked her crooked cigarette. Signs posted everywhere said, "No smoking."

"Oh right, the *big* secret project that you can't talk about?" Lunette mocked.

"Lunette, we've *never* been able to talk about this. I don't know why you're even making it a thing right now," she said, walking through the plaza, looking up at Sequentia headquarters, the angular glass office building towering over the rest of the smaller buildings in the office park.

"Sorry, geez."

Aimee didn't respond as she stubbed out her cigarette near the big bronze statue of the company's founder, a large-framed, bespectacled man in a well-fitting three-piece suit that stood in front of the building where she worked.

"Aimee?" Lunette asked after a long pause.

"It's muggy as hell out here," Aimee responded as she walked past the guard napping at his post.

"I can't stand the heat," Lunette said sympathetically.

As Aimee passed through the automatic door, the sliding glass scissored open with a quiet whisk, the blue lights inside enveloping her as she crossed over from the warm, humid air outside into the air conditioning.

"The lab has the best AC," she said as she walked down the interior hallway. "They keep it so cool here."

"Aimee! I thought you were leaving!"

"No, I was taking a smoke break and needed to

vent. I'm going back into work, and I'm taking you with me into the lab. I want you on the phone with me."

"Using me as an excuse if you get ambushed by Marky again? So you aren't even going to pretend to try to make that date, huh?"

"Lunette," Aimee joked, "didn't you hear what I told you? I'm on the verge of a breakthrough."

Her sister paused for a second. "I knew it!" Lunette said and cackled.

"Just shut up and come with me," Aimee said, as she passed through the cold hallways of Sequentia to the lab where she worked.

Bromancing the Stone

Somehow, much later, after they'd trudged as far up the beach as they could go, way past any real civilization, Darnell and Rod came to a rock-wall-backed private beach. They sat there in silence for a while, absorbing the atmosphere, the sound of the crashing waves, and the way the moonlight suffused the beach. For the next thirty minutes or so, they sat there pondering the effects of the mysterious tea they'd consumed.

They waited.

They gazed around, wondering when it would hit them.

The night seemed normal enough.

"Maybe if we lay down?" Rod asked.

"In the sand?" Darnell asked. "I hate sand."

"Dude, let go a little. Come on," Rod said as he laid down.

"I guess," Darnell said, and followed. They stayed

there for a bit while the sound of the waves crashed in the background.

"Did that tea work?" Darnell asked after a moment. "I don't feel anything."

"Just wait," Rod said.

"It's been half an hour."

"You don't feel that?"

"Feel what?"

"Just stop complaining and listen."

"Listen to what?" Darnell's voice rose in annoyance.

"Shhhh!" Rod said.

The two of them went quiet and looked back up at the sky.

It looked absolutely huge, a giant bubble of light and stars around them.

The rhythmic lapping of waves filled their senses until all they could hear were molecules of water moving about with billions of others, and it calmed them. And all of a sudden, to their surprise, they both realized they were in a very pleasant state.

The moon perched high above them, cartoonishly large and bright. The stars were a twinkling net spread across the sky like pixie dust.

Rod sat up, followed by Darnell. They were both feeling euphoric now.

"*Ulp,*" Rod burped and gulped at the same time.

Darnell gulped and burped simultaneously as well.

They gave each other urgent looks, and Darnell put a hand to his mouth. Rod did the same. They both stood up and ran to the ocean – its crashing waves were swirling colors that were thick like paint. The landscape was bending before them with every step, while the sand dunes of the beach around them looked gigantic in the moonlight.

Darnell doubled over first, releasing the contents of his stomach onto the beach. Seeing him evacuate his stomach so violently, Rod quickly followed suit.

A few moments of wet, retching noises from both of them, and then ...

There was silence for a moment.

When they stood up they both felt renewed.

Lighter.

They both stumbled away from the edge of the ocean and made their way back up to the dry sand.

Everything had transformed.

Or had it?

They looked at each other. The sky was a spectrum of colors that swirled and expanded with their breath. Time seemed to slow and collapse, then to stop altogether. In this breathing bellows of warped color and perception, Darnell and Rod struggled to remember a time when they hadn't felt this way.

"What are we doing here? Were these trees always moving like this? Why did we come up here again?" Darnell didn't even know if he was speaking English.

"There was something ... I can't remember," Rod said. "Something I was trying to forget."

"Are we doing it?" Darnell asked, his voice light and trailing away. "Have we done it?"

"Who knows, man? I don't even know if I'd 'done it' even if I'd done it," Rod said.

Darnell sighed in response. "Well, what's next then?"

"I don't know. But I like it out here. Away from all the cameras and screens," Rod said. "Even in stupid Pop's Diner, in a remote place like this, I couldn't get away from the news. But here with the trees and the waves and no people. It's nice."

Darnell nodded. He reached into his pocket and pulled out his phone. The rectangular screen lit up in the dark. He looked at his calendar. The screen could have been mistaken for a cubist painting, and meetings were indicated by colorful squares to show which hours were booked.

Every moment of every one of his days was already spoken for.

"I feel like this calendar controls my life," Darnell lamented. "I hate how my whole life is laid out in blue squares on this stupid screen," he said, and shook his head. "Is that what all this amounts to? My life laid out in little blue squares on a screen?"

The waves lapped at the rough sand. The gray Atlantic was cold, huge, and unaffected by Rod and Darnell's tiny concerns.

"These things are stupid," Rod said pulling his phone from his pocket. "It's all such annoying nonsense. Noise."

"I can't remember the last time I didn't have a phone on me," Darnell said.

"Let's get rid of them," Rod exclaimed.

"Really?" Darnell asked.

"Yeah! This stuff was supposed to 'show us the way.' This must be the way!"

Rod tapped his phone angrily.

"I hate everyone on this thing," Rod said of his phone. "Everyone on it is always talking about money I owe them."

Darnell looked surprised.

"What did you just think about?" Rod asked.

"I hate all these people on my phone too!" said Darnell.

"I know! Fuck this shit!"

"Yeah!"

"Throw them in the ocean!" Rod cried.

"Okay! What?" Darnell asked, suddenly unsure.

"On three! One, two, three!" Rod cocked his arm and threw his phone far out into the choppy Atlantic. Darnell hesitated for a moment, then tossed his phone out into the dark water in a lazy arc. The two phones made distant splashes, and Rod cried out in victory.

"*Woohoo!* We're breaking the cycle!" Rod whooped in celebration.

Darnell laughed as well, feeling giddy.

"This is exciting," he said happily.

"It *is* exciting!" Rod exclaimed. He reached in his jacket, whipped out a pistol and started shooting in the general direction of where their phones landed. "Fuck the government! Fuck the police! Woo!"

Darnell was nerve shatteringly startled. "Rod! Whoa!"

Rod squeezed off a few more shots.

"Rod! Please!" Darnell cried in terror and annoyance.

"What?" Rod asked in confusion.

"Dude, goddamnit," Darnell said like an old granddad, "I was just starting to have fun. Give me that thing."

Rod handed over the gun sadly.

"I've got a license," he said lamely. "It's for protection."

"From your phone?" Darnell replied caustically. "You've already drowned it."

"It was just a burner," Rod replied.

"Wait, that was just a burner you threw in the ocean?" Darnell asked.

"Yeah. What? You threw your real phone in the ocean?" Rod asked. "What about your contacts?"

"Yeah! What about my contacts!" Darnell exclaimed.

Darnell snatched the gun from Rod, and after checking to see if it was loaded, slipped it into his jacket.

"You keep trying to stress me out, Rod," Darnell said in dramatic fashion. "I'm on your adventure, but please don't keep stressing me out like that."

Rod shrugged and tried to look guilty in the moonlight.

Down out of the woods, floating through the clear air over the sandy beach, Darnell heard the soft notes of a jazz band drifting through the night. The music calmed his jangled nerves a bit.

"Do you hear that?" He asked Rod.

Rod cocked his ear. The smooth sounds of a big band came from somewhere in the woods: the pluck of the bassline and the lilt of the horns.

"Where's it coming from?" Rod asked. "I thought we were alone out here."

"I don't know," Darnell said. "But it sounds like a party?"

"A party, you say?" Rod asked. "We should go check it out!"

Up the beach, the border of the forest looked magical in the moonlight. The trees reached up and shifted in the night air, while the leaves rustled in the wind that blew in off the ocean. The rainbow-colored undertones of shifting light pulsed with faint jazzy notes. The leaves and undergrowth seemed to faintly glow a light purple, and the woods seemed strangely inviting.

"Let's go," Rod said, and set off wandering up the beach toward the forest and the music. "Let's see who's responsible for these silky smooth stylings."

Darnell followed, sucked in by the seductive quality of it all.

Rod crossed beneath the canopy and into the woods.

Darnell looked back once more at the moonlit beach and the stars in the sky. Their footprints stretched away in the sand. Their tracks leading up to the woods looked lonely under the immense sky – the small indentations in the sand were the only sign they'd ever been there at all.

For a second, he thought he saw shadows of himself and Rod walking on the beach, their feet falling exactly where their footprints already lay in the sand. But then it was gone.

He turned to follow Rod, leaving the dreamlike beach and entered the shadowy forest.

The Doorway

"What were we talking about?" asked Aimee as she walked into her frigid laboratory. She was surrounded by machines: giant sterile, industrial monoliths that were stacked up around her.

"Just now?" Lunette asked. "Your personal life."

"And what about it?" Aimee asked, as she crossed the white linoleum-tiled main floor of the lab, white curved walls enclosed the ultramodern space.

"You look tired all the time," said Lunette, "and you're clearly lonely."

"Lonely?" Aimee asked. "You can really see it that easily?"

"Yes, Aimee," Lunette said. "Everyone can."

Instead of responding, Aimee's eyes sparkled in admiration as she reached the center of the lab.

On a large pedestal, inside a thick fire safety cell, was a machine that looked like a freestanding wall, white and wide, and standing about eight feet tall. On the bottom right of the machine was a crisply designed logo that read, "P10."

"What about your old boxing instructor?" Lunette asked.

"I mean, his class was good," Aimee said as she walked up to the flat surface of the main control station.

"I *bet* it was!" Lunette said.

Aimee reached into her purse and produced an oblong, ruggedized case bearing the embossed logo of Sequentia Labs. The logo was a depiction of a circle surrounding a kite shield, with the shield divided into four quadrants, each containing a symbol: a pickaxe, a sword, a quill pen, and a rose.

"It was good until his feelings got in the way," Aimee said absentmindedly as she focused on the case's locking mechanism. She pressed the lock with her index finger, and the hand-length clamshell case opened softly.

Inside, there was a small inner compartment containing a folded-up piece of ancient-looking parchment on the left and three compact pink-filament fuses on the right.

"That must be a luxury," Lunette said. "Aimee, I'm kinda jealous of you! You could have any man you want."

"People tell me that all day long. I'm focused on work," Aimee scoffed. "Is that such a crazy concept?"

She ran her fingers from the parchment in the left side of the case to the three fuses in the right side of the compartment.

The first fuse was a burnt-out husk – the sparkling filament inside had been destroyed, split down the middle and burned to black ash. The second and third fuses were delicate constructs, with their filaments still intact, pink and blue rays of bending light shining past the boundaries of their glass enclosures.

"Just chill out," Lunette said. "You never know. The next one could be great."

"I doubt it," Aimee responded, feeling the cold glass of the fuses beneath her fingertips.

"You're so negative. I love it," Lunette said. There were rummaging sounds in the background and what sounded like dishes clinking.

"What about you? Don't you have a hot date tonight?" Aimee asked.

"Nope. My date is with *Law & Lace* reruns and a cheeseburger," Lunette said. "On my couch, with a tall glass of rosé. Special Prosecutor Arturo Ricardo is just so cute."

The TV in the background of the call got louder.

"I don't get why people like that show. I've never watched an episode," Aimee chided her with a smile. Then she paused. "Lunette," she said in a serious voice, "listen to me."

"Oh dear," Lunette said. "This sounds more serious than your average afterwork chat."

"That breakthrough that I wasn't supposed to mention earlier," Aimee said, picking a working pink fuse gingerly from the clamshell case. "I'm nervous about it, and I want you on the phone with me."

"On the phone with you for what?" Lunette asked as Aimee left the case on the control surface. She walked down past the controls and crossed through the foot-thick wall of the safety barrier surrounding the P10.

"For support," Aimee said.

Inside this smaller chamber, Aimee walked up to the pedestal upon which the gleaming white machine sat, right in the center of it all. There was an opening, a small cradle in the center of the face of the machine into which she plugged the fuse.

It fit perfectly into the cradle with a well-oiled click.

"You're breaking up, Aimee," Lunette said.

"I think it's going to work this time," Aimee said. "I think my calculations were just a little off last time."

Aimee stepped down from the pedestal surrounding the machine and left the shield barrier enclosure.

"I can barely hear you. You think what's going to work this time?" Lunette asked, her voice losing some of its previous humor.

"Give me a second, Lunette," Aimee said, as she pressed a chunky button protruding from the barrier housing's surface, engaging the vacuum seal on the chamber.

Outside the barrier wall, she walked back to the control surface and instinctively picked up the clamshell Sequentia case. She leaned over the large control surface and touched one of the glowing orange options to trigger the machine.

The filament gleamed in its glass housing as it

warmed up. It began to glow, slowly at first, pulsing. The blue-white light it emitted grew unevenly in intensity, dipping from blinding to dim, only to flip back in the blink of an eye, until it began to grow more consistently in brightness and intensity.

"What's that noise?" Lunette said, but her words were distorted. "The phone's making a crazy noise."

All of a sudden, a focused beam rocketed out of the glowing filament, shooting patterns of neon-pink light onto the walls and ceiling and floor of the shielded test chamber.

As Aimee watched the fuse heat up in the machine, she ran her hand across the ruggedized case and looked at the clock.

"Well, the opera's intermission would just be ending by now," Aimee said as she turned up the power. The P10 hummed louder, generating more heat.

"It's past the intermission, and you're still worried about that date? Let it go. He's either long gone or watching the play by himself."

"Maybe he met his future wife. You never know."

The lab rumbled as the chamber reached critical temperatures, but still Aimee had not gotten what she'd hoped for.

"Aimee, you sound like you're in the middle of a jet engine," Lunette said. "Are you okay?"

"I'm *fine!*" she said loudly over the ruckus as she upped the intensity once more.

She could smell the hot circuits.

Static from the overworked processors made the hair on the back of her neck stand on end.

The machine was creating so much heat that beads

of sweat began to appear on Aimee's brow. Lunette was saying something on the other end of the phone, but she seemed small and far away.

"Aimee! What the hell is that sound? Are you alive?" Lunette screamed into the phone.

The containment chamber lit up like a star.

The filament inside the fuse vaporized into ash as it burned out.

And she heard a pop, like a little bubble bursting.

As the P10 finally overheated and burst into flames, it was immediately extinguished by foam jets in the containment chamber. Aimee felt a presence looming over her shoulder and turned to confront whatever had appeared behind her.

"Lunette," Aimee said, in a hoarse whisper. "I think it worked."

"Aimee! You're still there? What the hell was that?" Lunette panicked. "I'm freaking out here. That noise sounded like the world was ending."

Behind Aimee, a wooden door had appeared in the wall. It had a heavy iron knocker twisted into a strange shape.

"No, Lunette. Not the world ending," Aimee said.

"What was it?"

"It *worked*," Aimee said.

"The thing you've been working on all these months? Really?" Lunette asked, excitedly. "For real? Aimee! That's amazing! What is it?"

Aimee's heart started beating faster. With the remaining fuse inside, she closed the Sequentia case with nervous fingers, and stuffed it back into her purse. She cautiously walked up to the strange door and ran her hands over its rough wooden surface.

Her eyes shone in anticipation.

"It's a door," she said. "An old wooden door."

"'An old wooden door?' That's what you've been working on for months? Shouldn't it at least be a new wooden door?"

"It just appeared," Aimee said.

"Now you sound crazy," Lunette said worriedly over the phone. "A door 'just appeared'?"

"Yep."

"So what are you gonna do?"

"I think I'm going to go through it," Aimee said as she placed her palm against door.

"Aimee," Lunette said, "do not go through that door."

Aimee pushed the heavy door in.

It swung slowly on old creaky hinges.

"Were those creaking hinges?"

The world on the other side of the door was dark.

"Don't do it!" cried Lunette.

But Aimee ignored her. Beautiful, haunting jazz music wafted out of the open door as she ventured through it. On the other side was a bed of thick, well-maintained grass and dark, mysterious shadows.

"I hope you didn't just go through that door, Aimee! I know I heard hinges creak! And what is that music?"

"Don't worry, Lunette, I can always turn around and go back. It's a door; it works both ways."

"A door that just appeared! What if it disappeared

just as easily?"

"It's fine," Aimee said, though her heart was beating faster. She'd crossed fully over into this darkened world but still had a hand on the door, holding it open.

"You're here on the phone with me," Aimee said.

"Kind of! I mean, it keeps breaking up," Lunette said to Aimee. "Aimee please don't go in there!"

But Aimee didn't listen.

"No, Lunette, I'm going to see this through."

Following the jazz that floated through the air, Aimee let go of the door.

"At least drop a pin!" Lunette said frantically.

"Fine," Aimee said, and opened up the menu on her phone. "Hold on, let me put you on speaker."

The wooden door began to slowly swing shut.

"Aimee?" Lunette asked, as the shaft of light coming through the door began to narrow. "I hear the hinges creaking again! Is the door shutting?"

"Hold on, I'm doing it, Lunette," Aimee said as she prepared the pin with her location.

The jazz from the big band seemed to swell as the shaft of light shrank further.

"Aimee, you're breaking up," Lunette said. Her voice sounded heavily garbled now.

Gripped by a moment of doubt, Aimee made a quick motion back toward the closing door to try and stop it. But she was too late.

"Aimee … re you ther … ?" Lunette's voice stuttered, as the door clicked shut, leaving Aimee in the dark.

Lunette's voice cut off, and the phone went silent.

The door had disappeared without a trace.

Aimee looked down at her phone and saw that it had no signal.

"For real?" she muttered. She locked her phone on the pin of her last known location and slid it into her purse. Then she turned in the direction the jazz music was coming from and began walking, high-stepping in her heels across the soft bed of grass.

Her long day wasn't over yet.

Trippin' Out

Huge maples and big beech trees towered over Rod and Darnell. In the darkness, reality seemed stretched a bit thin.

Jazz music echoed through the woods. The faint notes flitted in and out of earshot, as they both stumbled forward on rubber legs, attempting to work out the correct direction to walk in.

"Do you think it's real?" Darnell asked in a quiet voice. His feet looked like they were melting through the ground.

"What?" Rod asked, who was also concentrating on not sinking into the forest floor. "The music?"

"Yeah," Darnell said, looking at the swaying trees surrounding them, entranced.

"Well, you hear it too, right?" Rod asked, trying to find his fingers.

"I do," Darnell replied honestly.

"Then it's got to be real," Rod surmised. "We can't

both be hearing the same music unless it's real."

"Let's go with that."

They trundled on across the forest floor, feeling like they were on an adventure to discover some lost ruins or a strangely inaccessible tree fort. The trees surrounded them, their old and solid trunks bending to and fro quietly in the night.

"Can I tell you something, Darnell?" Rod asked.

"What is it?"

Rod paused for a moment, gathered his thoughts as best he could, and found there wasn't much to gather. He'd lost the thread.

"What, dude?" Darnell asked again.

"I can't remember," he said to Darnell. "I feel like I've been here forever …"

His voice trailed off. He was feeling overwhelmed by all the colors blooming around him.

Despite their remote location and the lateness of the hour, the woods around them felt inviting. Blooming colors swelled all around them as if they were a miniscule part of some endless organism. Darnell opened his mouth to say something, but before Rod could hear what he had to say …

Everything shifted.

Darnell looked up at the canopy of leaves and branches high above them.

They formed a kaleidoscope of shapes and light before his very eyes. The whole world looked like it was folding in on itself over and over again. He was struggling to keep the thread.

Rod was talking about … something.

Darnell could hear his voice, but it was muted. He couldn't understand a word, but Rod kept talking, and slowly but surely, Darnell was eventually able to hear things around him again.

"I think I just had a little episode," Darnell blurted. "I saw … something not real."

Rod looked at Darnell with an eyebrow arched.

"Yeah, sure you did. Tell me about it."

Darnell began to talk, but Rod stopped him.

"No. Stop. Don't really tell me about it. You should remember it though. It may mean something." He walked on dismissively.

Darnell followed as Rod kept moving forward. They came over a rise, and the music got louder.

Notes were rippling out through the night like raindrops in a pond.

"What is that!" Rod exclaimed as they both gawked.

There was, in the near distance, a red and faintly glowing thing. It pulsed scarlet light into the darkness, a bizarre large bush with strangely twisted roses growing on it. There was something slightly unnatural about the way its petals spiralled.

"It's a rose bush, I think," Darnell said. "But I don't know why it's glowing like that."

"That's the drugs," Rod said.

"You think so?"

"Oh yeah. For sure."

"Is it glowing like that for you too?"

"Yeah man! Let's go check it out!" Rod said and scampered forward.

"So if we both see it, it must be real, right?" Darnell muttered as he trotted off after Rod toward the dark-red light of the bush.

"Maybe this is what I've been looking for." Rod barged onwards.

"You've been looking for a glowing rosebush?"

Rod didn't hear him but looked back over at Darnell to say, "Come on."

He walked right up to the bush, his face glowing in the light. He reached out, mesmerized, and tried to pluck a flower. As his fingers closed about its stem, a long wickedly hooked thorn pricked his finger.

"Ow!" He exclaimed and quickly drew his hand back.

"Are you okay?" Darnell asked, walking over.

"Yeah, I just cut my finger," Rod said. He looked down at his hand and saw blood welling up out of the gash. A fat red droplet wobbled and fell, splashing onto the glowing petals of the rose.

The music swelled louder, sounding closer than before. Rod sucked at his wounded finger.

"What's that?" Rod asked, around his bleeding finger. "Over there."

He gestured beyond the rosebush. Down an old path, they could see a faint twinkling of light.

"I don't know, but I think that's the direction the music is coming from."

"Let's go see."

They left the glowing rosebush to follow the golden light.

Meetings by Gaslight

"Do you remember how we got here?" asked Darnell.

They stood before a hedgerow which seemed impossibly high. The wall of leaves was tightly manicured, huge, and ludicrously green. The music floated over from the other side, lilting and tempestuous all at once in that beautiful way that only jazz can be.

There was a lamppost.

And a doorway.

The lamppost was an old, black iron thing, elegantly wrought to resemble vines growing, with a gas flame enclosed in a brass-and-glass fixture that illuminated the doorway in a pool of syrupy yellow light.

The door was set into the lush hedgerow, and was a solid wooden construction, adorned with a heavy iron knocker that was twisted into some strangely awkward shape. The two gazed at it as if it had landed from space.

"No. Did you know this was here?" Rod asked quietly.

The music in the air was faintly magical; a cool breeze stirred the leaves in the trees.

The gaslight flickered around them.

Darnell didn't reply.

His pupils were dilated to the size of dimes. When he spoke, his voice sounded innocent, almost childlike.

"Hey Rod, why is there blood on your hands?" Darnell asked.

Rod's pupils were so big, his irises looked like black holes. He looked down at his hands and saw a smear of blood glistening in the light from the lamppost on his index and middle fingers. He looked back at Darnell.

Rod chuckled, sounding a little unhinged.

"Don't you remember?" he asked Darnell. "The rose."

"Oh yeah," Darnell said, his eyes widening. "The rose."

"Dude, is this shit coming off?" Rod asked. A slight tinge of panic crept into his voice as he scrubbed at the small smear of blood with his other fingers and a dab of saliva.

"Rod. You're fine," Darnell said calmly. "Don't worry about your finger. Let's talk about this crazy door here."

Rod and Darnell stared at the door.

"What the hell is it doing way out here in the

middle of nowhere?" Rod asked.

"I don't know," Darnell replied. "I was under the impression there was nothing out here on this property."

"Really?"

"Really."

"Well," Rod said, "this night was supposed to be all about change."

He smiled at Darnell, who gave him a piercing look.

"Rodney, you can't just go through strange doors and expect your life to be changed," Darnell said.

"Maybe. But you can't know that unless you try it," Rod grinned as he spoke.

"Let's just say I'm making an educated guess," said Darnell. "Plus, this isn't our property. We're probably trespassing."

"I haven't seen any 'No Trespassing' signs. Have you? And aren't you coming out here to survey this stuff tomorrow?" Rod asked.

"We must've gone too far. This must be the neighbors' property."

"So the neighbors are throwing a party? This music is basically an invitation!" Rod exclaimed enthusiastically.

"Hearing the music to someone else's party is definitely not an invitation. You can't just burst into any party you want to, Rod," Darnell advised.

"That's not what life has taught me," Rod said. "Doors are made to be walked through. I never saw a door I didn't at least try to open."

"I'm not sure your privilege is allowing you to see this clearly."

"You're just as fucked up as me!"

"So?" Darnell asked. "I'm still acting more rationally!"

"Says who? Maybe going through that door is the most rational thing in the world, and right now you're being irrational by saying we shouldn't."

Darnell folded his arms. "Rod, do you hear yourself?"

"Come on," Rod said petulantly. "Are you ninety years old, Darnell? Has it come to this?"

"No, you c'mon, Rod. Do you really think going through this weird-ass door in the woods is a good idea?" Darnell asked.

"What's the worst that could happen?" Rod asked gleefully.

"Don't say that! Terrible things can and do happen, all the time."

Rod's hand grasped the strange, twisted knocker, and for a split second, it glowed bright red. The music seemed to pause for a breath. Colors swirled in their vision, and the whole world seemed to inhale. Rod pushed on the timbers of the heavy door, his bloody fingers leaving prints on the wood, soaking into the dry planks. It swung inward on heavy iron hinges.

The music swelled.

Darnell and Rod passed under the lush hedge, the earthy smell of growing plant life surrounding them and crossed through the opening.

The hallucinations from the tea immediately stopped, and the scene around them unfolded beautifully.

The path on which they found themselves was made of smooth paving stones and was well lit: it was lined with lampposts that cast yellow gaslight. Small shrubberies and benches made of iron and wood also lined the path as it meandered across the lawn and eventually made its way up the hill to an enormous and stately old manor. The house's windows may have been lit up gaily, but the structure itself was a dark, hulking silhouette: old, quiet and knowing.

"So good of you to make it," a smooth voice said from the darkness under a nearby tree. The voice belonged to a handsome, well-dressed man who was sitting in the shadows on a bench, babying a filterless cigarette, its tip glowing a hot red in the cool night air.

The man's face was like a statue: he had strong features and skin with no blemishes. His hair was dark brown and oiled down, and one perfect curl was draped down over his forehead between his sleek brown eyebrows.

He wore a slim, fitted black suit, black leather shoes, a white button-up, and a narrow black tie. The tie was fixed to his shirt with a thin gold clip. He dropped his cigarette and stood, crushing the butt under the toe of his pointy black shoe.

"Come. Join the other guests. New people and new perspectives always liven up a party. After all, a party is only as interesting as its guests, no? I'm David, by the way," he said with a slick smile.

"I'm Rod," Rod replied. "And this is Darnell."

"Well, come along then," David laughed. "The

party awaits."

He turned and beckoned for them to follow.

Rod and Darnell looked at each other, shrugged, then fell in behind David as he began to stroll up the long, gaslit path to the house.

Rod tugged on Darnell's sleeve and mouthed, "Do my eyes look crazy?"

"They look fine," Darnell whispered. Darnell pointed at himself, and Rod nodded too. They both looked totally normal, no appearance of hallucinogenic effects.

"Are we still tripping?" Rod mouthed.

Darnell shrugged.

Off to their left was a beautiful open pavilion, a marble-tiled square with delicate cascading terraces of flowers surrounding it. A large group of partygoers, all drinking and laughing, gathered beneath strings of electric lights.

On a low riser, an outdoor ten-piece band played the wonderful jazz tunes they heard floating into the night. Directly in front of the riser, couples swayed together rhythmically to the music.

"Hey, can we go over there?" Rod asked.

David smiled. "Let me show you to the house first. There's plenty of time yet for you to mingle, dear Rodney."

"How late is this party supposed to go?" Rod asked earnestly.

"No plans to stop any time soon," David said. "We're not the type of crowd to cut a party short, shall we say?"

"Nice!" Rod said happily.

"And is this your house?" Darnell inquired.

David smiled, his perfect teeth sparkling. "No, it belongs to a wonderful family. Mr. and Mrs. Gilbreth and their young daughter Penny. I'll introduce you if I see them. They're around here somewhere."

"So what's the occasion?" Darnell asked. "I'm surprised at the scale of it all!"

"It's a very special night for the Gilbreths," David said happily.

"Why?"

"Come, find out for yourself," David said smiling at him.

They left the pavilion behind and worked their way up the hill. Beautiful people littered the great lawn around the house, all enjoying each other's company, in fantastic fairy-tale surroundings.

Women in ornate dresses sipped champagne, while people around them laughed and babbled sweet nothings. A dishevelled man holding a bottle of alcohol attempted a cartwheel in the crowd, and everyone around him laughed and egged him on. A few couples slipped off into the darkness, to make love amongst the flowers.

"It's lovely, is it not?" David asked. "The sprawling chaos of a good party?"

"I couldn't agree more," Rod said, distracted by the spectacle of it all. "I love a good party. I'm so glad we found this place. Last time I wandered in the woods high on drugs, it ended up way worse than this."

Darnell just took it all in, looking around in silence.

"Look at all this splendor," David said, gesturing at the party unfolding in front of them.

"Somewhere, in all that chaos, someone is raising their glass to toast some beautifully trivial nonsense. Some fleeting promise being made with there never being any intention or real expectation of it being fulfilled." David's eyes sparkled, and he seemed quietly animated as he spoke about the party. "No butterfly was ever as rare or endangered as a sincere promise made at a party after three a.m."

They followed David up the steps to the front porch, his hand trailing on the heavy oak bannister that ran alongside. Nearby patrons turned to greet them as they crossed into the fold. They passed people wearing faces of drunken joy as they reveled in each other's merriment. David wore a strangely satisfied smile as he looked back.

"Here we are, my new friends," he said happily. "Welcome to the party!"

Welcome to the Party

The painted front door of the house swung in on great, brass hinges when David pushed it. He shepherded Rod and Darnell into the house, coaxing the thick, colorful crowd in the foyer to part for them.

The main hall was a cavernous room with walls that flew up to vaulted ceilings, a huge ballroom-like space, like some cathedral of pleasure. Lights in ornate, worked-metal wall sconces and in massive, complex chandeliers hanging from the vaulted ceiling lit the room in a pleasant golden light.

In the center of the main hall, perched high up on a pedestal in a space cleared out on the dance floor, was a naked, statuesque woman lit up like an angel by a spotlight. The tall, fit woman wore a blonde bob wig and all around her, in a giant mass, was an orgy of naked partygoers, all writhing in pleasure below her, reaching up, trying to caress her legs.

"Hell yeah, this is fantastic," Rod exclaimed happily.

The three stopped just outside the foyer at the edge of the main hall, standing in a row, shoulder to shoulder in the crowd, and looking into the gorgeous chaos of the party that unfolded in front of them.

"Odessa Gilbreth," David said, pointing to the center of the main hall, at the woman on the pedestal above the orgy.

Darnell and Rod were unable to look away from Odessa.

"Niiiice," Rod said, and grinned like the Cheshire Cat.

"Oh ... wow?" Darnell said, stupefied by the scene in front of him.

To the right of the dance-floor-turned-orgy in the main hall, a twenty-piece big band played atmospheric music to accompany her moment in the spotlight.

Two giant ascending staircases mirrored each other as they curved and climbed up through space to the second floor, framing the orgy below. People gathered all around in this beautifully appointed expanse, holding cocktails, congregating in groups, chattering inanely.

And watching.

Most of them were watching.

"What am I even looking at?" Darnell exclaimed once he'd recovered his faculties. "I can't believe what I'm seeing!"

"Dude, don't ruin it," said Rod.

Several other members of the party shushed

Darnell as well, and David smiled paternally as Darnell slapped a hand over his mouth and looked a bit ashamed.

Odessa looked over them all from above, women caressing women, men pleasuring other men, women and men together in all different configurations pleasing each other while trying to please Odessa as she watched, naked, from on high. She reveled in their writhing pleasure. An overweight man lying on his back and touching his throbbing member as he waited for an elusive partner looked up at Odessa and winked.

"I can't ... " Darnell sputtered.

"Please, Darnell! Be cool," Rod said under his breath.

"Don't worry, my new friend," David said. "Everything is just as it should be."

The sea of flesh mingled together. Heads and bodies bobbed in the background. The odd couple, momentarily excited to climax, would moan or scream out in pleasure, then the sound would dissipate, leaving the sloshing and slapping of hard cocks and the rubbing of slippery fingers against nubile skin. As a whole, very little detail could be made out, save for a flash of hair or the parting of waiting lips.

Off to the side of it all, two fiery, red-haired artists on scaffolding were painting an enormous portrait of Odessa's naked body. The two young women were twins and naked themselves, with paint smudged across their pale-skinned bodies. They looked at Odessa with fervent adoration in their eyes.

"They're so ... beautiful!" Darnell said, watching the two twins dance across the canvas.

"So you see something you like?" David asked, laughing good-naturedly.

Darnell's eyes followed the two slim, naked forms as the women painted with vigor.

Using dramatic colors and bold strokes, they had rendered Odessa's form onto the gigantic canvas as she was, perched upon a white marble pedestal, her sculpted legs dangling down into the pool of copulating partygoers that sprawled below her.

"Dude, this is the best place you've ever taken me, bar none," Rod said. "This is just what I needed right now. I love you, dude."

"I ... love ..." Darnell was just staring like a lost puppy at the naked twins, overwhelmed at all the bare flesh around him, so he wasn't able to respond properly to his friend.

"I know, dude," Rod said, and clapped Darnell on the back. "It's okay, I know. The first time is crazy!"

Darnell was having trouble containing his amazement.

While they watched, Aimee slipped up between them all.

"This is some weird shit, isn't it?" she commented.

Startled, Darnell looked at her and said, "Damn, you scared the shit out of me."

"That scared the shit out of you?" she asked. "You must startle easily."

Rod chuckled. "He does have bad nerves."

"My nerves aren't bad!"

"Rod, Darnell, I see you've met Aimee." David

leaned over and said, "Aimee, this is Rod and Darnell, our newest party members."

"What do you think about all this?" she asked, gesturing to the painting and orgy they were watching.

"I love this place," Rod said without irony. "It's been a while since I've been to an orgy this big. It doesn't even smell. Amazing."

His eyes gleamed.

"I wasn't expecting … all this!" Darnell exclaimed. "I'm a bit startled."

"It is a bit startling," she said, and they both laughed.

"I was supposed to be enjoying a nice, quiet weekend in the woods," Darnell said, unprompted.

"Well, if it makes you feel any better, I should be on a date at the theater right now," Aimee said with a wry chuckle.

"What happened?" Darnell asked.

"I got a better offer," Aimee smiled, and looked Darnell in the eye. Darnell looked away.

"Better indeed," David said happily. "I'm sure your date would've paled in comparison to this." He smiled. "Where else would you find company like this?" he asked.

"Hell yeah, where would you randomly find company better than this?" Rod asked loudly, grinning at the party all around.

"Okay, well, hold on a second there, buster. I'm not totally sure about the company yet," Aimee said flatly. "I don't know any of you people."

She looked around.

"And who's to say my date wouldn't have ended better than this? Don't be so quick to judge," she said and gave David a pointed look.

He smiled at her, unfazed.

"I like her," Rod said.

"That's great," she said and folded her arms. "You want a cookie?"

Odessa laughed aloud as one particularly enterprising partygoer tried to climb the pedestal to reach her. She pushed the naked man off with her bare foot, and he landed in the pile of writhing orgy participants before being subsumed into the thrusting, seeking, moaning pile. Her straight, white teeth sparkled in the spotlight.

"She's so beautiful," Rod said in awe.

"That's one word for it," Aimee said.

"She is rather statuesque, isn't she?" Darnell remarked innocently.

"Statuesque?" Aimee asked dryly.

"Oh yeah," Rod interjected. "Super statuesque."

Aimee shook her head. "Gross. All men are the same," she lamented.

David smiled and patted her on the shoulder.

"Just relax," he said to her. "We're all the same when we're boiled down to our basest desires, men and women alike."

"I suppose," she said. She looked at his hand as he patted her.

"Do they take volunteers?" Rod asked David.

"Of course, dear Rodney. But you must ask Odessa

for permission," David replied.

And Aimee rolled her eyes.

Odessa ran her hands up her ribs slowly, enjoying her body, and cupped her breasts in the spotlight, posing for the two artists, as the young women feverishly produced their rendering of her image on the nearly story-high canvas.

One of the artists stretched herself out to plant swaths of color in out-of-reach places on the massive portrait. The other one flicked paint off long brushes to add to the image.

"Darnell, what were you saying about the twins right before Aimee showed up?" Rod asked.

"Yeah, Darnell, what were you saying about the naked young twins right before I showed up?" she asked, looking directly at Darnell.

"Uhhh," Darnell began, "I was just saying …"

"Yes?" she asked.

"How beautiful they are?" Darnell finished.

"*Are* they?" She gave him a pointed look. "Like Odessa?"

"Well, yes. I think, anyway," Darnell said, blushing furiously.

The crazed look in Odessa's eye seemed to glow hotter and hotter, as she reveled in the exaltation. All around her, her little minions were pleasuring each other to worship her at a more fevered pitch, and she was clearly aroused by the experience.

Odessa cried out in pleasure and laughed in delight, as the four of them watched on, each with mixed emotions.

"Well," Aimee said, as it all wrapped up. "This has

been … interesting."

"That was awesome!" Rod said. "I love exhibition-
ism!"

"I'm staggered," Darnell said, his eyes wide.

David laughed, and clapped him on the shoulder.

"It's good to see someone still so innocent in this
jaded world," David said cheerfully to Darnell. "You're
a rarity, that's for sure."

The marble pedestal was quickly wheeled from
the dance floor. The twin naked artists and a group
of orgy participants moved the gigantic painting of
Odessa behind the main bar.

Partygoers moved back onto the dance floor and
closed the gap that Odessa and the pedestal had left.
The orgy participants slowly melted away into the
crowd, and put their clothes back on. The big band
played on as pretty girls danced and drank opulently
decorated tropical drinks. Men stood around, smiling,
sipping bourbon and artlessly boasting about alleged
larger-than-life accomplishments.

Beautiful dancers dressed in full burlesque sauntered through the crowd and grabbed the hands of
revelers as they passed, dancing provocatively with
men and women alike, much to the partygoers' delight.

Clouds of smoke hung above them.

The gaggle of fervent adorers that surrounded
Odessa dressed her in a gray velvet dress, attending to
her every gesture. They seemed to move as one with
her. After they had dressed her and departed, a cruelly
beautiful man with raven hair, jet black eyes, and a

three-piece suit, who'd been waiting, moved to speak with her as she neared the bar.

"Come," David said leading Rod, Darnell, and Aimee from the edge of the foyer toward the epicenter of the party at the main bar.

"Odessa will want to meet you," he said grandly, smiling as he walked into the crush of the party.

Odessa

A large, circular dais rose up from the floor between the ballroom's two mirrored crescent staircases. On top of the dais there was a giant, ornate wood-and-marble bar. The back of the bar was a pyramid of liquor bottles that jutted like a crown above the swirling mass of partygoers below. Glasses clinked and the smell of cologne and perfume mingled with the laughter and good humor permeating the atmosphere.

The gigantic, detailed painting of naked Odessa was now in place behind the bar, towering over the whole party.

"Odessa!" David called over the crowd, leading Aimee, Rod, and Darnell through the bedlam, across the floor, and up the wide, flat steps of the dais. "Odessa!"

She turned regally toward him from where she stood at the bar. She looked over, away from the tall, raven-haired man she was speaking with, and gestured

"One moment" to David as she ended her heated conversation.

She looked resplendent in her platinum-blonde wig, with her face covered in thick makeup and her gray velvet dress trimmed tastefully with gold accents. Large gold-scale earrings dangled in sparkling cascades from her ears, and her pointed shoes were twinkling gold as well.

She radiated a worldly, experienced air. When she walked, her athletic frame undulated, shoulders and hips floating separately from the liquid, elegant movement of her long legs.

The man she'd been talking to was very pretty, with a square jaw, clean-shaven, with his raven hair beautifully dishevelled. He wore a stylish, three-piece suit, and had a gold watch fob that ran to his breast pocket. He pouted when she walked toward David and his group at the other end of the bar.

The pretty man glared at Aimee and looked away to order a drink.

"Odessa," David said, "I've turned up some new subjects for your kingdom. This is Rod, Darnell, and Aimee."

He gestured to the three.

"Oh goodness! I love meeting new guests!" She looked at Aimee. "This one, I've already met. But I still love this purse."

Odessa trailed her fingers across Aimee's small, black purse as she brushed past her to talk to Darnell and Rod with her hand held out limply to be kissed.

Rod grabbed it.

She pulled it back. "Not so fast," she said, looking

him in the eye. Odessa smiled, and turned to Darnell. "Your friend here isn't rushing. It's a party. Relax, take your time," she said, running a nail delicately down Darnell's neck, sending a shiver down his spine.

She gave Rod a broad, satisfied smile. She lowered her eyelids at him, and her eyes smoldered. "Pleased to meet you, darlings." She held out her hand again, dangling it limply at the wrist, and aimed it in Rod's direction.

Rod took her hand again, bowed over it for a moment, and then landed an overly familiar kiss atop it.

"Hm. Maybe I *do* like you," Odessa said, smiling at Rod. "And you, dear. Cheer up," she said, shifting her cold blue eyes to Aimee. "You look so serious. It's a party after all."

Aimee frowned slightly and stood up straighter.

"There you are. You look better already. You cut quite the figure," Odessa remarked, looking Aimee up and down, noting her long black hair and her stylish black dress. "These fools will go crazy over you to be sure. Just remember, you'll have more control over them than they ever will over you. Never let them bully you."

Aimee's mouth was slightly open as she absorbed this. "I don't quite know what to say," Aimee replied.

"Then say nothing, dear, but keep your mouth closed. We don't need to see all that gawping."

Aimee clicked her teeth shut.

"It's like a fairy tale," Rod said with stars in his eyes.

"Yeah," Aimee said dryly. "A big booze-soaked

fairy tale."

"Except this is no fairy tale," Odessa said dryly. "I pride myself on being a realist, and what we've achieved here is nothing short of a miracle."

Darnell looked at her in disbelief.

"But this is just a party," Darnell said.

"Just a party," Odessa scoffed. "Bah! What do you know?" She turned to Rod, and slapped her hand on the bar. "Get me a vodka tonic, love," Odessa said to Rod.

The giant bar and pyramid of liquor behind it lit Rod's face up as he flagged down the bartender.

"Vodka tonic, love! And a whiskey neat. Make it a double," Rod called to the bartender and leaned his elbow on the wide, granite bar top as he waited. He smiled at Odessa.

"Oh God," Darnell said. "He's really going for it."

"What do you mean?" Aimee asked.

"I can tell by the look in his eye," Darnell said.

The bartender delivered Rod the drinks, and Rod disbursed Odessa's while he sipped his own.

"Here you are, my dear," Rod said to her. "A drink, to the most beautiful woman in the room."

"He's laying it on thick," Darnell whispered to Aimee. "I told you."

"Oh, Rodney," Odessa said, as she took the drink. "You're such a shameless flatterer."

"Have I flattered you shamelessly enough?" Rod asked Odessa. "Are you intrigued by my mysterious ways?"

She smiled.

"Oh, I don't see much mystery about you, Rodney," Odessa replied in a sultry tone. "But I would surely unravel you, just to say I did."

This House is Weird

"This house is weird," a gravelly woman's voice said in a thick German accent. A diminutive lady, with short, graying hair, and thick glasses walked up to the bar between Odessa and Aimee, and ordered a drink. She turned to Odessa.

"What?" asked Aimee.

"You look beautiful as always, Odessa," the woman said, ignoring Aimee completely.

"Thank you, Klara," Odessa said. "I do appreciate the kind words." Klara waited at the bar while the bartender mixed her drink, and Odessa gave her a sidelong look. Aimee was looking a bit put out by Klara's interruption.

Klara turned her icy gray eyes, magnified behind her thick, gold-rimmed spectacles, on Aimee and smiled.

"Odessa is always fantastic," Klara said to Aimee.

She gestured round the room with her drink. The party was lurching along under its own momentum all around them, the enormity of the main hall echoing every merry sound, magnifying it.

"And this house," Klara continued. "Isn't it beautifully built? It's like a castle, but made out of wood."

"I guess so?" Aimee said, uncertainly.

Klara continued over Aimee as if she hadn't heard her.

"Old Man Percival built this thing all the way out here for a reason," Klara said in her guttural voice.

"Who?" Aimee asked.

"Old Man Percival. Have you not heard his story?" Klara asked in a mysterious tone and continued before anyone could answer. "He was a visionary! He risked his family and fortune in Europe on an expedition to the New World. And he found something on this land," Klara said ominously. "Or rather, deep beneath it."

"What did he find?" Aimee asked, intrigued.

"Whatever he found, he built the family residence right near the place where he discovered it."

"Okay, Klara," Odessa said, no nonsense. "That's enough."

"Okay, okay," Klara said in a mild, conciliatory tone. "I won't bother your pretty, young guests anymore." Aimee gave Klara an odd look. Darnell shifted awkwardly and buried his expression in his drink. Rod smirked a little.

"Thank you, dear," Odessa replied in a patronizing tone.

Aimee jumped at the sound of champagne bottles popping nearby as a knot of people celebrated something vaguely defined, cheering for some fleeting idea that would probably not last the night.

"That startled me," Aimee said to Darnell and laughed, placing her hand over her chest.

"Look whose nerves are bad now," he said, laughing along with her.

She shot him a dirty look. Before Klara could move away from their group, the pretty, raven-haired man who had been talking to Odessa earlier slipped up beside Aimee and grabbed her by the bicep. The party swirled around them, and no one noticed, but Aimee's eyes grew in anger as she turned her glare on him.

"Trevor!" Aimee exclaimed furiously. "You *dick*! Never ever grab me!" The party didn't miss a beat.

"You ran off so quickly when we were speaking earlier," Trevor said, in a slimy voice. She tried to jerk her arm from his grasp, but he would not release her. "I ran off because you're a creep! You don't know when to stop!"

Darnell was looking angrily at Trevor, and Rod and Odessa turned to face him too. Odessa was looking supremely furious.

"I know when to stop. I didn't do anything untoward," he said creepily. Odessa moved closer to Trevor.

"Trevor!" Odessa yelled. "Let her go!"

Trevor dropped his hand from Aimee's bicep immediately. Even unrelated members of the party froze for a moment at Odessa's bellow.

"You always single out the newest, youngest

woman at the party!" Odessa shouted. "Why must you always be such a lecherous pervert?" Trevor's face turned beet red, and he shrunk down into himself as if the words were physical blows.

"What did you to this young woman?" she continued. "I bet she wasn't here five minutes before you got your grubby mitts on her."

"I didn't d—"

"Shut up!" Odessa rode over his meek voice like a thundering locomotive. "Do not bother her or us again!"

Eventually, he could take no more and slunk away into the crowd. The people closest to them all glared at Trevor in tandem with Odessa, as if her eyes directed their collective gaze.

"All of this is so terribly boring," Odessa said to Aimee. "Let's dance."

She turned, with Rod's hand in hers, and began to move toward the dance floor. The crowd around them all parted to let her through.

"C'mon," Aimee said to Darnell. She rolled her eyes and laughed. "Let's get this over with."

They all ran out into the rhythmic melee of the dance floor.

Do Not Interrupt

They all went to the front of the dance floor and began dancing directly in front of the band. The two pairs danced along to the music, Aimee with Darnell, and Rod with Odessa. Rod grabbed Odessa, and she laughed as the two danced to the music, with the crowd around them always deftly moving out of Odessa's way.

"It's been a long time since I've done anything like this," Darnell admitted. "It feels nice dancing with you."

"I hate feelings," Aimee replied. "They're just … not logical."

"Really?" Darnell looked bemused.

The tune the band was playing shifted into another soft melody, and they continued to sway to the back beat.

Darnell smiled.

"What do you do?" Aimee asked Darnell while

looking around during a slow part of the song.

"I'm a lawyer," Darnell said.

"What about you, what do you do?"

"I'm a scientist," she stated flatly.

"So, what's your favorite number?" Darnell asked incongruously.

"I tell you I'm a scientist, and you ask me what my favorite number is?" she asked, focusing coldly on Darnell's face.

"Oh, I didn't know that was a sensitive subject." Darnell looked down. "Where do you work then?"

"42," Aimee said under her breath.

"What?" Darnell asked confused.

She smiled. "Never mind."

Rod swayed with Odessa across the dance floor.

"I gotta say," Rod said in Odessa's ear during a particularly close moment. "Your body is amazing."

"Oh is it?" she said, sounding intrigued.

"It sure is," he said, and pinched her bottom.

She didn't miss a beat dancing but pulled his hand firmly from her and held it in an iron grip.

"You are uncouth," Odessa said to Rod, glaring at him.

"You love it." Rod smiled and drew her closer to him. "All the ladies do."

"Oh, do they?" she remarked. "I'm not 'all ladies.' Do I need to train you?"

In response, he twirled her to the beat, and the conversation ended. The moment of slight tension passed, and they both laughed like it was the funniest thing in the world.

"That asshole," Aimee muttered in disgust when she noticed Trevor skulking toward them, his pretty face twisted with petulant anger. Darnell glanced over his shoulder and saw who she was looking at.

"Let's just get out of here, then," Darnell said to Aimee.

"Fuck that, I don't run from my problems," Aimee said.

Trevor walked up to Rod and Odessa. She gave him an icy look.

"May I cut in?" Trevor asked them in a greasy tone.

"Absolutely not," Odessa spat.

"I'm so sick of this fucking guy," said Rod.

Trevor gave them a shallow bow and smiled before he turned to Darnell and Aimee.

"C'mon, man," Darnell said, annoyed. "You're really going to ask?"

Trevor looked directly at Aimee and asked with a smile, "Might I cut in on this dance?"

"Go away, Trevor," Aimee said. "No one wants you here."

"Just listen to her," Darnell said.

Trevor stood still, looking stiff and upset.

Rod looked at his angry face and then turned to Odessa. "Hold on a second," he told her.

"What?" Odessa asked.

Rod boogied over to where Trevor stood and said, "Kind sir. May I have this dance?"

"What?"

"Surely you've danced before?" Rod interjected.

"Never with a man," Trevor said as he looked

up and down at Rod with disgust. "What are you, a dandy?"

"C'mon baby," Rod smiled. "You worry about labels?"

Rod quickly grabbed Trevor's hands and began swinging them wildly with the rhythm of his dance moves. Trevor forcefully tried to pull himself away but was unable to, and as the dance went on, his face grew redder with rage.

"Let. Me. Go," he said in a voice full of venom.

Instead of complying, Rod swung Trevor's hands harder and got closer to him as he danced around. And just when Trevor could take it no longer, Rod pinched Trevor's butt. Trevor pushed Rod away and was able to break his grasp, but not before Rod turned around and began rubbing his butt against Trevor's crotch.

Trevor let out a guttural cry of rage before he stepped back and took a swing at Rod, who easily dodged it. Trevor overextended himself, which threw him off balance. He teetered on one foot for a moment, then fell into the band with a crash: the horn section at the front scattered, and the string section in the back retreated from the calamity.

The music unceremoniously stopped.

Everyone turned and looked in horror.

People began rudely slinging comments from the back of the crowd.

"What the hell happened?" someone yelled angrily.

"Yeah, what the heck is going on?"

"Where did the music go?"

Odessa rounded on Trevor with murder in her eyes. The people nearest her turned on him, too, mirroring Odessa's rage, their features twisted into savage expressions.

As the band picked up their fallen instruments, Odessa strode directly to Rod and Trevor.

Rod opened his mouth to speak.

She held a hand up and cut him off before he even began.

"You," she said, pointing at Trevor, malice burning in her eyes.

Trevor tried to scurry off into the crowd, but Odessa caught him by the collar.

"You think you can run away that easily?"

Before he could respond, she cut him off.

"What do you think you're doing, Trevor? I don't care much if you're an asshole. But I do care if you start to wreck the party. *My* party."

"I'm …"

"This is *my* party!" Odessa shouted at him. "I'm the reason *any* of us are here."

"Bu—"

"No buts!" Odessa said. "All I want to hear from you is apologies, you *dog*."

"I'm sor—"

"I don't *care* about your feeble apologies," Odessa spoke over him. "You know the *rules*, don't you?"

"Yes madam," Trevor said, trembling as he kneeled before her. A circle of angry, jeering partygoers surrounded him in support of Odessa.

"You *know* the party is *never* to be interrupted!"

"Yes madam," he said, his eyes trained on the floor.

"And yet here we are," Odessa sneered, leaning over his cowering form. "Because of your bungling actions."

She lifted a long, beautiful leg, placed her sharp high heel on his shoulder, and kicked his kneeling form over backwards.

"You disgust me," Odessa said, as Trevor scrambled to his feet.

"I'm sorry, madam," Trevor whined, grovelling.

"Get out of my sight. You are less than nothing," she said coldly.

Trevor skulked off into the crowd like a whipped dog. Odessa and the mass of partygoers surrounding him all watched his every step as he slunk away.

"Now *you* three," she said ominously, turning to Darnell, Aimee and Rod.

"I know you're new here, and because of that, I'm going to be lenient. But mark my words well. *Do not interrupt my party!*" Odessa's voice grated in her throat with anger. "Consider this your only warning. There will not be another."

Good Times

"Everyone! Your attention please!" Odessa called out to the crowd on the dance floor, stepping out in front of the band. The band started back up and the string section held a tense note as she gathered the crowd's attention.

"Thank you all for bearing with me through these slight hiccups," she said, her voice ringing out over the dance floor. "If you would all follow me out onto the lawn, there will soon be a fireworks display for your enjoyment."

A ripple of excited chatter ran through the crowd at the news. The band changed to a happier tune but still played it at a low volume as the crowd absorbed the information.

As the crowd reacted, a stately old white couple in immaculately tailored clothes walked up to Aimee, Rod, and Darnell. The woman wore a fashionable but conservative blue dress, had a pillowy cloud of white hair, and was draped in diamond jewelry. The handsome, old, silver-haired gentleman standing next to her was wearing a checked blue jacket and white slacks with boating shoes.

"Well ... that was quite the display," said the dapper old man. "I'm Arthur Longfarthing. This is my wife Mary."

"I'm Aimee," said Aimee since she was standing closest to the old couple.

"He doesn't look much fun," Rod whispered to Darnell.

"I love the way you dance!" Mary Longfarthing said brightly to Aimee, chiming in like a little fairy godmother. "Would you like to come watch the fireworks with us?"

"Mom, leave them alone," said a slightly drunk young man as he walked up, his chinos rumpled and his button-up crinkled. "Can't have our newest guests watching the fireworks with all these *old* people."

"Benjamin!" Arthur said. "Be polite to your mother and the new guests."

"Dad, come on, they don't want to go listen to your dusty old stories of how you got your start," he said, laughing, his cheeks red and ruddy from drinking. "They want to have a good time. They're going to come drink and party with Isetta and me."

Arthur Longfarthing harrumphed.

"Come with us," Benjamin said to Darnell, Rod, and Aimee, as his wife Isetta walked up beside him, smiling. She was a mousy young lady, freckled, wearing a cute muted-beige dress. Benjamin looked at her, and they smiled at each other.

"We have the perfect place to watch from," Isetta said to Aimee, grinning.

"Okay," Aimee said.

Benjamin led them across the lawn and over to the side of the house to a black iron ladder in a semi-circular iron cage that led upward.

"Wait, you're serious?" Aimee asked. "We have to climb that ladder?"

Benjamin smiled at her mischievously.

"There's no way I'm getting up that thing in my dress and heels," Aimee said.

"Don't worry!" Isetta said. "It'll be worth it."

"Fine. Well, I'm going last then," Aimee said, adjusting her purse. "Otherwise, you pervs will be looking up my dress."

They climbed up the ladder and ended up on the rooftop, a red-clay-tiled terrace surrounded by a waist-high wrought iron railing.

"See," Benjamin said, waving his hands, gesturing out over the grand expanse of the party. "Up here, we're closer to the fireworks."

Below them, the iron gas lamps that dotted the lawn, the strings of lights that hung above the pavilion, and the lights on stage with the outdoor ten-piece band all combined to make a magical bloom that illuminated the merriment before them.

"This way, we'll be right up close when they go off," Benjamin said as Darnell and Rod and Aimee all took in the view, their faces underlit by the light from the lawn below.

"There's wine up here too," Isetta said, walking over to a cask that was up on the roof. "We hid it up here earlier." She smiled.

"You dragged that whole barrel up here?" Rod asked.

"Well, Benjamin helped me," she said. "I mostly just carried the glasses."

Aimee looked at the ring on Isetta's finger.

"You're so young to be married," Aimee said, as Isetta filled the long-stemmed glasses with wine. "I can't even imagine getting married so young. I still can't even make it to a date on time."

Isetta looked warmly over at Benjamin.

"With Benjamin, the choice was easy," Isetta said, smiling at him. "We've been in love ever since we first laid eyes on each other."

"And what about this place?" Aimee asked. "Do you two like it here?"

The music from below reached the roof in faint waves, like a beautiful memory.

"This place is fine, but I'm really only here because my parents were weirdly insistent I show up to this party," Benjamin said to the three. "We don't really come to their parties. It's not our scene."

"Yeah," Isetta piped up, "this crowd is all the Gilbreths' friends. But Mary told me, 'Make sure you two show up for this party.' I don't know why it was so important."

After Benjamin and Isetta handed out tall glasses of deep-red, aromatic wine to everyone, they rearranged the seats on the roof to make a horseshoe shape so they could sit and take in the fireworks.

The band started a new tune.

Boom!

The first shot flew high into the air and exploded, scattering thousands of white sparkles across the sky.

The fireworks lit their faces as they looked upward.

"Fireworks are always good," Darnell said.

"You know what else is good, Darnell, old friend?" Rod gulped a large swig of the viscous red liquid in his glass. "Old friends." He gave Darnell a stupid smile and pointed at him.

"You're drunk," Darnell said.

"I may be drunk, but you're beautiful," Rod said looking at Darnell first, then turning to Aimee.

Aimee gave Rod a look of surprise. Darnell just rolled his eyes.

"Are you hitting on me?" she asked Rod, incredulously.

"Are you single?" Rod asked.

"Single?" Isetta asked butting in.

"You're not together?" She asked Aimee and Darnell.

Aimee's face reddened. "Him?" Aimee pointed at Darnell and laughed nervously.

"Yeah!" Isetta said. "You two are so cute together!"

Aimee looked at Darnell. "No," Aimee said flatly.

"What's the matter?" Rod asked. "You don't want a boyfriend?"

"Why would you even think I want one?" she asked. She stood up and moved so that she was addressing the group to the backdrop of the fireworks.

Boom!

The blast of a firework mortar behind her was followed by crackling fingers of color high above them, brilliant fingers of light spread in every direction.

"Everyone assumes that I need someone," Aimee said, "that I need a man or a relationship to make my life mean something."

She took another deep swig of dark red wine.

"My family? Society?" Aimee railed against the night sky, her hands in the air. "Well, let me tell you something. They are *all* wrong!"

She pointed firmly at Rod, then Darnell and Isetta to emphasize her point.

"I can do whatever I want! Why is it so hard for people to understand that?" The color was rising in her cheeks. "I don't need another person. It seems like anyone I allow into my life somehow puts me in a position I'm uncomfortable with. The only way I like it is when *I* call the shots."

She closed her eyes and began to move to the music of the band. She swayed rhythmically back and forth in her slim black dress, silhouetted by the blasts of the fireworks that lit the sky behind her. She lifted her half-full glass to the sky as it sparkled from the light of the explosions.

"I'm fine by myself," she reiterated, then sat down.

The group was quiet for a moment, absorbing the lights and colors of the fireworks.

After a while, Darnell remarked. "How beautiful it all is. The fireworks almost look like stars."

"Stars!" exclaimed Isetta in disbelief. "We haven't seen stars since …"

Benjamin grasped her hand and squeezed, and she went silent.

"Ever since what?" Darnell asked.

They didn't answer.

The fireworks ended, and after a while, Rod asked Benjamin, "That was nice, but what should we do next?"

Benjamin took a long swig of his wine and swirled it in his cup. He looked at Rod for a long moment before replying.

"Well ... there is a secret bar," he said.

"A secret bar?"

Benjamin nodded. "On the second-and-a-half floor."

"There's a second-and-a-half floor?" Aimee asked.

"There is indeed a second-and-a-half floor," Isetta said, as if she were telling them the final clue to a murder mystery.

"How do we get to the second-and-a-half floor?" Darnell asked.

"Over there," Benjamin said. He pointed to a hatch that opened in the floor of the terrace.

Rod looked at Aimee and Darnell. "You want to check it out?" Rod asked.

Aimee looked at Darnell, who shrugged, and they both nodded.

"Will you come with us?" Aimee asked Benjamin and Isetta.

"No, you go on," Benjamin said, hugging Isetta to him.

"We're going to stay up here and drink a while," Isetta said and smiled.

"Wanna go?" Aimee asked Rod and Darnell.

"What have we got to lose?" Rod asked as they walked over to the hatch.

The Long Hallway

Aimee opened the hatch and ducked inside, followed by Rod and then Darnell. They descended the ladder, down the dark chute from the rooftop terrace to the second-and-a-half floor. Shadows surrounded them as they stepped off the ladder and onto the dark wooden floorboards below.

The hallway before them was lined with burning oil torches that left little black streaks up the golden walls. Great arched pillars of aged, oaken beams in the walls held up the ceiling. They could see a door down the hallway at the opposite end.

"Are we sure this is the way?" Aimee said, looking down the hallway.

"You sure this area isn't off limits?" Darnell said. "Ya know? Mansion parties. If we get caught, it might be bad ..."

"Nowhere is off limits at mansion parties," Rod declared.

"I'm not sure that's true," Aimee said.

"Look, I don't have time to go over this," Rod said. "I'm going down this hallway to that door!"

"Rod! Wait!" Darnell exclaimed.

Before he could stop him, Rod marched away down the hall.

Aimee turned for a moment to look at Darnell, then made a sour face as she followed Rod. As she walked away from Darnell, with her black purse bouncing behind her, she called over her shoulder, "Hey, don't you want to see what's on the other side?"

The door was shaped like a spade pointing upward; otherwise, there was nothing interesting about it. It was just a plain, white, double door. Above it was a sign molded out of golden metal which read, "The Secret Bar."

"Oh, it's a bar," Rod said drunkenly. "I eat bars for breakfast."

"It seems to me bars eat you for breakfast," Darnell shot back.

Rod made a raspberry noise and bounded the last few steps to the entryway beneath the sign. Just before he was able to enter the bar, he was stopped by a heavily muscled man who looked squeezed into his suit, who had seemingly emerged from nowhere.

The bouncer was wide-shouldered and tall, and wasn't threatening-looking, just blocking the way with his extremely wide shoulders.

"I'm sorry guys." The bouncer's voice was high-pitched and sounded incongruously kind and sweet coming from his rugged frame. "Only people that have paid the cover can get in."

"What! You aren't gonna let us get into your stupid secret bar?" Rod asked.

"You have to pay the cover," the bouncer said as he rolled on his feet.

"What's the cover?" Darnell asked.

"I'll need a secret from each of you," the large man said, looking pointedly at them. His suit made a strained sound from the continual effort of holding back his muscles.

The three looked at each other for a moment.

Rod was the first to speak. "I once had sex with a transexual!" he boasted loudly. "And I *liked* it!"

The other three all looked surprised.

"Okay, thank you. That's enough," the bouncer said.

"Don't knock it till ya try it," Rod winked.

The large man shifted slightly uncomfortably in his suit as Rod moved out of the way.

Darnell walked up next, and cleared his throat. He paused for a moment, and then spoke as if he was addressing a courtroom. "I ... once cheated on my taxes." He made to enter the bar, but his path was blocked, and he bounced off the bouncer's rock solid muscles.

"That's not a secret anyone cares about," the bouncer said dryly.

"Uh," Darnell said, taken aback. He recentered himself. "Okay. I once went swimming, at night, in a public pool, after they'd locked the park."

The bouncer just looked at him, expressionless.

"Naked?" Darnell offered.

"No." The bouncer said flatly.

"I fed my ex-girlfriend some pork dumplings once, and told her they were vegan." Darnell tried.

"Nope." The bouncer wasn't impressed.

"I once stole a car?" Darnell offered.

"Are you asking me?" The bouncer asked.

"No." Darnell said.

"Then no." The bouncer said. "Your secrets bore me." He looked annoyed and folded his arms.

"When I first got my license, the first time I took the car out, I backed over my neighbor's cat and then blamed it on my grandma," Darnell said in an anguished, hesitant voice.

The bouncer thought for a second and then said, "Fine, I'll take it."

"Can't believe you never told me about that," Rod said in surprise as Darnell joined him under the golden sign to the bar.

Aimee walked up where Darnell had been standing. She stood up on her tiptoes and leaned in close to the bouncer, until her lips were almost touching his ear. She whispered something softly. Upon hearing it, the bouncer's eyes widened, and he looked at her in surprise before stepping aside. "What?" she asked Rod and Darnell. "It's all about what you got."

She patted them on their shoulders, shook her head, and crossed under the sign into the bar.

Rod looked at the bouncer, then at Darnell, and then back at the bouncer.

"This guy ..." Rod gestured at Darnell.

The bouncer shook his head in agreement. The two followed Aimee into the bar.

The Secret Bar

When they entered the room, they took in their surroundings for a moment, before walking over to the wooden bar. The room was panelled in gold leaf; the bar's surface was milky white glass, lit from inside so the room glowed with its light. A giant rectangular mirror behind the bar reflected their movements.

"This floor feels cozier than the rest of the house," Aimee said.

"Yeah, all the gold-leaf panelling makes the room feel small," Rod said.

Aimee and Darnell looked at him skeptically.

"What do you know about 'gold-leaf panelling'?" asked Aimee.

"Just something my interior decorator told me once," Rod replied.

Aimee, Rod, and Darnell all leaned against the bar near where they entered. Aimee ran her hands across its smooth, glowing surface as it illuminated their faces from beneath. Rod smoothed his hair as he looked at his reflection in the giant rectangular mirror behind the bar.

"I like this," Aimee said. "How the liquor behind the bar is lit up from below."

"It feels like a luxury cave or something," Rod said, looking up at the light on the ceiling, which was refracting like a sparkling pool through the liquor bottles.

A woman with fiery red hair in a bright-red dress sat further down the bar, away from them, her features softly underlit – she was drinking a martini that glowed when she placed it on the bar.

"That's one of the painters from earlier!" Darnell said in awe.

"The ones that are 'sooo beautiful'?" Rod said in a mocking voice.

Darnell looked sheepish.

"Who's that guy talking to her?" Rod nodded at a dark-haired man next to her. The man was wearing a crisp suit and a rakishly angled hat, and he was hovering aggressively over the painter.

"Watch this," Rod said and ambled down the bar to the red-haired woman.

"Hey hey! How's it going down here?" he asked loudly, making eye contact with the man.

"Hey, hey, yourself, buddy," the stern-faced man said. "Why don't you beat it?"

The woman looked at Rod to see how he would react. Rod just smiled at her, then looked directly back at the man and said, "No."

The man blinked in surprise, as the painter smiled into her martini.

"No, right?" Rod looked to the red-haired woman for reassurance. She nodded at him.

Rod looked back at the man.

"No," Rod repeated. "It's the lady's choice, so I'm sticking around. Wanna buy me a drink, Mr. Cardboard?"

The man stared daggers at Rod for a moment, then stood up and walked up the bar toward the exit in a huff, barging past Darnell and Aimee on the way. Rod turned to the painter and asked, "Can my friends sit here?"

"Sure they can."

"I'm Rod by the way."

"I'm Sinead," she said, flashing a dazzling smile.

"Your painting is amazing," Rod said. He motioned for Aimee and Darnell to come down the bar and sit next to him and Sinead.

"I can't take all the credit. It's my sister's too," Sinead said.

"Where is your sister?" Rod asked.

"She's somewhere around here. We're supposed to meet up soon," she said. Sinead watched in fascination as Aimee walked over. "You're so beautiful," she said to Aimee before anyone could say anything else. "Come sit, over here by me."

"Oh, thank you!" Aimee said smiling. "I'm not nearly as beautiful as you are!"

"You're a dear," Sinead said as Aimee sat down

next to her.

Just as Rod was about to introduce Darnell, another beautiful, red-haired woman burst into the bar down at the entrance, laughing loudly.

"He can never handle my secrets," said the new woman chuckling to the bartender as she ordered her drink.

Sinead leaned forward over the bar.

"Fiona! Over here!" She beckoned to her sister to come over.

"There you are!" Fiona said. "Look at all the friends you've made!"

Fiona strolled down to them, trailing her finger along the bar.

"Everyone, this is my sister, Fiona," Sinead said.

"Hi, I'm Darnell," he said, as he was closest to Fiona.

"You're cute," she said. She rubbed his bald head, then kissed the top of it, leaving red lipstick on his brown skin. He blushed.

"This is Aimee and Rod," Sinead added. "Aimee is clearly the hot one, and Rod here rescued me from some creep who wouldn't stop talking to me. And he didn't objectify me once the guy left!"

Sinead gazed at Rod.

"This one is pretty, I'll give you that. Not as pretty as his friend," Fiona said, running a finger down Darnell's chest.

"What?" Rod asked incredulously.

Fiona brushed past him.

"But this one," she said, moving to Aimee's other side. "She *is* the hot one. My dear, you look devastating in that dress."

"Nooo," Aimee protested, "you two are too sweet, I'm not that pretty."

Fiona looked at Sinead mischievously.

"Is it possible she doesn't know?" Fiona asked her sister.

"It seems that way," Sinead said.

"Shame," her sister said. "Confidence is such a turn on."

They drew closer to Aimee, complimenting her and touching her hair and face as Aimee laughed nervously. She leaned out from between the two twins and tapped Darnell on the shoulder.

"I'm going to the bathroom for a second, can you entertain these two?" she asked him.

"Oh no! You're not leaving us here," Sinead told Aimee. "We're coming *with* you!"

The gaggle of ladies all went off to the bathroom.

"I wish they'd stayed," Rod said. "Or even better, invited me to go with them."

"C'mon," Darnell said to Rod, "it's no big deal. Get you a drink."

"I kind of want a gin sling," Rod said.

"Can we get a gin sling for my friend here?" Darnell asked the bartender.

When the drink was set in front of him, Rod turned to Darnell. "You doing okay over there?"

Darnell toyed with his drink. "I'm okay. I just feel a little out of place at this party …"

"You've made that clear."

"And in my life really."

"Oh. Okay, what do you mean?"

"Like, my grandmother left me this enormous house that used to be all full of family. Everyone's gone, and I never got married and had kids of my own. I feel like I failed my grandmother."

"Hey, it could always be worse." Rod chuckled morosely. "The guys I owe money to are probably going to kill me next time I see them, and I'm going to try to put that moment off as long as possible."

Darnell laughed sadly.

"If the house makes you unhappy, you ever think about selling it?" Rod asked. "You could always help my broke ass out!"

Darnell stopped laughing and gave him a sharp look.

"No, I never think about selling it. And if I did, how would I live if I gave you all the money?"

"What if I could get you a production credit on my next movie?" Rod asked.

"It doesn't sound like there's going to be a next movie! No, I'm not going to sell my house for you," Darnell said.

Rod looked crushed.

"No?" Rod asked.

"No," Darnell repeated firmly.

"But, really?" Rod asked pitifully.

"Yes Rod! Really! I can't believe you even asked," Darnell said, then turned his back on his friend.

Aimee returned from the bathroom, sans twins.

"Guys. Those twins just asked me to have a threesome with them. One of them had some white powder. I think it was coke," she said to them.

"Did you do it?" Rod asked.

"Shut the fuck up, Rod," she said.

Before Rod could respond, David walked up and handed them a note. He appeared so quietly they hadn't even heard him arrive.

"I was given this by Odessa," David said. "She couldn't find you after the fireworks."

"By invitation only," Darnell read as he took the note. "You are officially invited to dinner by the Gilbreths' Fine Dining Society."

The script on the heavy card stock was very loopy and clearly written by hand with a fountain pen.

"And then there are instructions on how to get there," Darnell said, showing the card to Aimee.

"There isn't a time? And these directions don't make any sense," Aimee said.

"Don't worry about any of that," David said. "I'll take you there."

What Would You Do
To Live Forever?

David led the trio to a large dining room that was set off the main hall. Huge doors were slid back, and the room was wide open for people to come and go. The main dining table sat in the center of the room, an enormous heavy thing, wooden and creaking under the weight of all the silverware, drinks, and food. Long, buffet-style tables lined the walls.

A giant variety of things to eat were laid out on every surface of the dining room – every table was overflowing with a cornucopia of tasty treats: cherry-glazed roasted duck and dumplings stuffed with pig, basins full of ice and frothy bottles of beer, piles of red tomatoes and marbled steaks stained a deeper red with cooking wine.

Throngs of people served themselves from the enormous buffet along the walls, moving around a quartet of tubas that were stuffed in a corner at the back of the room, surrounded by food, playing lazy and slow music that could only be considered jazz, in that that it didn't ascribe to any particular style or sane rules. A core group of partygoers sat around the main table, in the center of which was a magnificent steer on a spit.

Odessa sat at the head of the table in front of dishes of ratatouille inside deep serving plates. The three spots to her left, near platters of crispy golden-baked chicken halves, were vacant. Trevor sat next to Odessa on the right side of the table. Next to him were Arthur and Mary, sitting in front of plates of Romano blocks that one could just pick up and eat. And then came Benjamin and Isetta, who were positioned next to serving plates full of browned pork chops seasoned with gravy galore.

Down the left side, next to the three vacant seats, sat Fiona and Sinead in front of a wide array of pies: pumpkin, cherry, Dutch apple, and lemon tart. The end of the table was stocked full of plates piled with buttery, flaky brown French toast squares still warm from the oven.

David led Darnell, Aimee, and Rod through the throngs of people as Odessa's voice floated through the hubbub. The flatly obtuse tones of the quartet of tubas pootled in the background of it all.

She waved to David. "Yoo hoo," she sang. "I saved you some seats next to me." She motioned for them to sit down next to her in the seats across from Trevor, Arthur, and Mary.

The partygoers in the room followed them with

their eyes as they walked down around the table.

"Right here next to me," Odessa said to Rod.

Rod sat in the seat closest to Odessa.

"I didn't save you a seat," Odessa said to David. "You never stay to eat."

"You know me too well," David said as he helped Aimee sit in her chair to the right of Rod, scooting her seat in for her as she sat. Darnell then sat to her right as David left the room.

Darnell ended up directly next to Fiona, who was smiling at him like she wanted to eat him.

"What's up with your band?" Rod commented to Odessa. "They sound like depression in motion."

Odessa said nothing but snapped her fingers, and the band picked up the pace with a more lively tune.

"We call it tubazz," she said.

"Oh?" Rod said, and reached for a pitcher of wine. He filled his cup to the brim, bloodred wine spilling over onto his knuckles as he sipped.

"So you're single?" Fiona asked Darnell as he filled his plate with French toast.

"You're no spring chicken," Sinead chimed in. "Have you ever been married?"

"Nope, but I got close once," Darnell said.

"Oh, Gina?" Rod asked.

"Yep, Regina. In high school. She was the love of my life. I literally thought we'd settle down and have kids."

"Awwww," Fiona said and rubbed his bald head. "You're so cute."

"I was just following my heart," Darnell said.

"Awwww!"

He smiled, and continued. "So I told my grand-mother about how I wanted to marry her, and even though she knew I was young and stupid, and proba-bly making a mistake, she supported me through the whole thing. She even gave me her grandmother's ring to give to this young lady."

"Darnell, you really are the sweetest," Fiona cooed and put her hand on his knee.

"So what happened?" Aimee asked.

"Yeah, what happened, Darnell? Do tell us," said Rod sarcastically.

"Well," he said, and looked at his ringless fingers, "it didn't work out. But my grandmother was my rock through the whole thing. I miss her."

"You poor baby," Fiona said.

Darnell shook his head. "I loved her so much," Darnell said to Fiona. "I wish she could've lived for-ever."

All of a sudden, Darnell stood up and raised his glass. Everyone at the table stopped what they were doing and looked at him.

"I have an important toast to make." He wobbled a bit and paused drunkenly. "To my grandmother," Darnell said, holding his glass in the air. "The fin-est lady who ever lived. If only she could have lived forever!"

"Hear hear," Rod said. "To Mrs. Walker."

Glasses twinkled in the yellow light of the gas lamps along the walls. They all clinked their glasses together.

When the toast was done, Odessa leaned forward,

and tented her fingers. "So, you wish she'd lived forever?" she asked in a strange tone.

"Yeah," Darnell said.

"What price would you have paid to keep her alive?"

"Oh," Darnell said, caught off guard, "I would've probably done anything to keep her with us."

Odessa smiled a deep and satisfied smile.

"We would do almost anything for our loved ones," she said. "But what about yourself?"

"What do you mean?" Darnell asked.

"I mean, what would *you* do to live forever?" she asked him. She focused her sapphire-blue gaze on each of them in turn as she spoke. "What would any of you do to live forever?"

Rod clamored over his friends to answer. "Oh, I'd do *anything*," he said.

"Anything, my poppy?" Odessa asked him.

"Oh sure," he said. "To live forever? I mean, wouldn't you, Darnell?"

Darnell thought for a moment. "It depends," Darnell said.

"On what?" Aimee asked.

"What would I have to do?" Darnell asked Odessa.

"Would you make a sacrifice?" Odessa asked him.

"Like an animal?" Darnell asked.

"I'd sacrifice an animal to live forever," Aimee said with no hesitation.

Odessa smiled and nodded.

"What kind of animal are we talking? Like a

chicken?" Darnell asked. "Or like an elephant?"

"You ask a lot of questions, my dear," Odessa said.

"What about a person?" Trevor said, casually.

"What?" Darnell and Aimee both asked in unison.

"Would you sacrifice a person to live forever?" Trevor asked.

"Yes, would you kill a person?" Arthur chimed in.

"Oh yeah," Rod said. "No problem."

"Rod!" Darnell and Aimee exclaimed.

The fairy-tale ambience of the room made for an incongruously cheery backdrop to this morbid conversation. The table was still swelling with luscious food, and the partygoers still picked at it as they talked.

"Depends on the person, I suppose," Aimee said. "Are we talking someone truly evil? I mean if they were really awful, sure, I guess. My mom? Probably not, depending on the day. And my mood. And her mood. You get what I'm saying." She took a drink.

"I couldn't kill anyone," Darnell said. "Not even if they were evil."

"I think you'd do it," Rod said to his old friend. "Just think of everything you could do if you lived forever."

"Like what? Spend an eternity thinking about how guilty I feel for killing someone?" Darnell asked.

"You'd be surprised how quickly you move on," Odessa said.

"Wait," Rod said. "You're telling me you actually killed someone?"

"Oh, Rod. Don't be foolish," Odessa laughed. "It's just party banter. What's a party without good conversation?"

The partygoers chuckled around the room, but Aimee, Rod, and Darnell stayed silent.

Poolside Manor

After dinner, Rod, Aimee, and Darnell escaped to the pool house. It smelled of chlorine and cigarette smoke. Partygoers in bathing suits ordered tropical-looking drinks. Drunken aquanauts in the pool splashed and frolicked, their laughter echoing throughout the tile-and-glass enclosure.

The three parked themselves at the end of the pool house bar. Soon, they were holding fresh drinks garnished with little cocktail umbrellas.

"Would you really kill somebody to live forever?" Darnell asked Rod as he took a sip of his drink.

"Yeah, pretty sure I would," Rod said.

"Yeah, pretty sure you're a fucking psycho." Aimee stirred then sipped her gigantic peacock of a drink. "You're just like them."

"No! I'm just not afraid to admit what I want!"

"Pretty sure admitting you'd kill someone to live forever means you're crazy," Aimee said.

"It is bizarre," Darnell agreed.

"Yeah, this place makes my head hurt," Aimee said.

"I know," Darnell said. "What the hell is even going on around here?"

"What is your problem? I love these people, they're a hoot!" Rod said. "I never wanna leave this place."

"What about the stars? You ever think about how we can't see them, or the moon here. I don't think those kids were joking," Darnell said.

"Who needs stars?" Rod asked.

"Not to mention that asshole Trevor," Aimee said. "There's a few too many things about this place that I don't like."

"Come on, guys. These wealthy people were kind enough to invite us into their private little world. We should be grateful that we even got to see any of this stuff," Rod said.

"I dunno. We weren't actually invited," Darnell objected.

"Yeah, I'm not sold," Aimee said. "I just want to get out of here. That last murdery conversation was the final straw for me."

"I agree," Darnell said.

"You're just two peas in a depressing pod," Rod said.

All of a sudden, a careening young man dove through one of the open window panels in the ceiling and hit the water of the pool with a great splash.

"What the hell?" Aimee asked, startled.

Rod looked up at the glass ceiling of the pool house and saw a few more young people queuing up on the roof above to leap into the pool below. They were jumping from the second floor roof through an open skylight. Each young man worked to outshine the last, escalating the complexity of the tricks they performed as they leaped.

"Those kids are fucking crazy," Aimee said.

"I can't even watch," Darnell said and looked away.

Aimee looked through the skylight that the young men were jumping through and caught the eye of a large, black man with muttonchop sideburns as he watched them from a second-story balcony.

Just then, one of the young men tried to execute a trick that was overly difficult and botched the jump. Instead of passing smoothly through the open window he hit the closed windowpane next to it.

"Oh my god, that's Benjamin," Darnell said, looking up when he heard the calamitous sound.

Spiderweb cracks ran through the glass panes under Benjamin's body, growing larger under his weight, as blood smeared from his lacerated hands and knees across the roof.

He tried to push himself up off the glass, but it gave way and shattered. He made no sound as he fell headfirst save a brief, high-pitched yelp and a crunch when his head hit the cement that surrounded the pool. The frolicking crowd in the pool house went silent as blood pooled on the pavement.

Darnell looked away, shuddering. Rod kept his eyes locked on the scene. People milled about, watching, but no one moved to help.

"I've got to get out of this fucking place," said Aimee, placing a hand over her mouth.

She looked up through the shattered and bloody windowpane, searching for the man standing in the upper floors.

The man with the sideburns was still there, watching, coolly detached from the situation below. His eyes were still locked on hers when he gestured for her to come follow him. Calmly breaking his careful observation, the man turned and walked back into the house and disappeared.

Not long after he was gone, two men from the crowd stepped in and dragged Benjamin off, leaving a dark, wet trail of blood. The rest of the partygoers went back to partying, and the crowd closed over the hole in the festivities.

"Man," Rod said, "that was fucked up. The way Benjamin hit his head."

"I know," Aimee said. "That sound ..."

"And the way the people reacted. It just doesn't make sense," Darnell said. "No one tried to help."

"Exactly. I'd really like to go now," Aimee said.

"Yeah, me too," Darnell agreed.

"Ehhh, don't be such party poopers," Rod said and took a sip from his giant drink. "I'm staying."

"Staying!" Aimee asked. "Seriously? A guy just died!"

"I saw two guys get shot at my old network exec's beach house, and the party went on for three more days," Rod said nonchalantly.

"Rod!" Darnell said on top of her. "What are you talking about?"

"Your friend is fucked up," Aimee said to Darnell.

"Yeah, I know," Darnell said, shaking his head.

"I'm right here you know," Rod said to her.

"I know," she said. "I kind of wish you weren't."

She pushed away from them through the milling crowd around the pool. "Ugh. I'm feeling sober now, and the smell of chlorine is killing me," she said as they caught up and followed her out of the glass pool house. "Let's get the hell out of here."

Clouds of Smoke

Darnell and Rod followed Aimee as she made her way back from the pool house to the main hall. People milled about the main bar, drinking and smoking, wiggling to the music, and rambling about their problems.

She walked to the edge of the dance floor and looked up to the second floor, searching. Darnell walked over toward her, but by the time he got to where she'd been standing, she was gone, as she had suddenly broken into a run across the dance floor. He followed after her with Rod in tow.

Darnell and Rod ran across the dance floor, fending off drunk women and frisky men, until they reached one of the main mirrored staircases that Aimee had just run up. They followed Aimee to the second-floor landing. They trailed behind her as she ran down the main hallway on the second floor, watching as she tried door after door to no avail.

"Hey!" Darnell said, running over to Aimee. "What are you looking for?"

"Did you see him?" Aimee asked, trying a locked door.

"Who?"

"That guy with the great big sideburns," she said urgently.

"Sideburns?"

"Yes, he was looking right at us."

"I looked away from the blood," Darnell said. "So, no, I didn't see him."

"He was looking down at us from the upper floors," she said, continuing to try more locked door handles. "He motioned for me to follow him."

"So what?" Rod said walking up. "What's that got to do with us?"

"I don't know!" Aimee exclaimed, obviously distraught. "I can't explain it, but he seemed … different."

"What does that even mean?" Rod asked.

She tried another handle, which was locked, and cried out in anger. "I don't know yet!" Aimee said. "But I feel like I *need* to find him."

"Some guy with giant sideburns … is gonna help us?" Rod asked flatly.

"Shut up, Rod," Darnell said. "Did you see him go this way?" he asked.

"I saw him turn the corner," she replied. "He must've gone through one of these doors."

"What do you want us to do?" Darnell asked.

"Help me find him," Aimee snapped anxiously.

Rod and Darnell started trying door handles on both sides of the hallway. After each of them had checked multiple doors, Aimee twisted a doorknob that turned. The door opened, and a huge wall of sweet-smelling smoke hit them as it billowed out into the hallway.

Aimee started coughing.

"Oh, hell yeah," Rod said. "This place gets better and better!"

Inside was a large, opulently furnished smoking room, where everyone was smoking marijuana, opium, and tobacco from different implements: hookahs, large ancient-looking pipes, and even animal horns. Huge purple velvet couches and chairs surrounded the room, and most of them were occupied by people who were smoking and laughing, lightly conversing, or quietly sleeping.

Rod entered the room first with a confident stride, and Aimee and Darnell followed him into the smoky den. Rod walked to the nearest open seat and plopped himself down. He smiled at the woman next to him, who smiled back and handed him a large wooden pipe.

"What's in that thing?" Aimee asked, still coughing as she sat in a chair across from the couch.

"Yeah," Darnell said sitting on the couch with Rod. "What *is* in that thing?"

"Who knows?" Rod said. "Tobacco at the very least, I'm sure. Maybe something fun. What could go wrong?"

He began puffing away at the pipe and immediately started coughing until he grew red in the face. "What is in this thing?" he asked the woman who'd handed it to him.

"It's a blend. Tobacco. A hint of tea. And opium, of course," she answered nonchalantly.

Rod looked back to Aimee and Darnell, and grinned. "Of course," he said, pointing to the pipe. "Of course it's opium."

"What are we doing in here?" Darnell asked Aimee.

"Relax, Darnell. Everything is going to be just fine," Rod said in a patronizing voice.

"You didn't answer my question," Darnell said.

Rod leaned back into the cushions of the couch.

Aimee didn't answer Darnell. She scanned the place with sharp eyes. In the recesses of one of the dark corners, the large black man with the mutton-chop sideburns was sitting at a table, smoking from a large wooden pipe.

He wore a brown leather motorcycle jacket, brown slacks, low leather boots, and was wedged between a man and a woman, taking long drags off the pipe being passed around. And he was staring right at her.

They locked eyes, both nodding slowly in recognition. He tapped out the bowl of his pipe and neatly set it on the table before walking over to where they sat. He didn't sit but kneeled and whispered to Aimee.

"We need to talk," he said, his voice deep and smooth.

"Can you help us?" Aimee asked him.

"I'm not sure yet," he said.

"Who *are* you?" she asked.

"I'm Raymond, and we can't talk here. There's an

old cabin near the back of the property. Just follow the lighted path until it forks, then take the overgrown trail. This trail isn't lit, but at the very end of the darkness, you'll find my cabin."

He turned and left the room before she could say anything, his large frame disturbing the smoke as he walked out.

"A cabin?" Darnell asked Aimee, when she told him what had happened.

"Another fucking cabin in the woods?" Rod exclaimed.

Darnell gave Rod a look, shaking his head.

Aimee got up and followed Raymond from the room without comment.

"Let's go," Darnell said to Rod, following behind.

"What?" Rod said, holding up his lit pipe. "We just got here. Can't I at least finish this?"

Darnell gave Rod a flat glare as Aimee left them behind in the murk of the crowd.

"Fiiiine," Rod sighed, and passed the huge pipe to the woman who had given it to him. He ran after Darnell who was already following Aimee out of the smoky room.

What Door?

Aimee coughed and waved her hands in front of her nose, trying to disperse the smoke as they stood in the long hallway outside the door to the opium den.

"Do you remember how you first got here?" Aimee asked when she caught her breath.

"Yeah, we came in down this hallway," Rod said.

"Not that," Aimee said, shooting Rod a dirty look. "I mean, do you remember how you first entered the grounds?"

"Yeah," Darnell said. "We came through a big wooden door in a giant hedgerow."

"A big wooden door?" Aimee asked sharply.

"Yeah, with a giant twisted iron knocker," Darnell said.

"And right after we went through it, we met David," Rod added. "He introduced himself and then walked us up to the main party, showed us around."

Rod turned to Aimee. "What does it even matter?"

She put her hands on her hips. "Can you take me there?" She asked and shot Rod a searching look.

"Back to the door?" Rod laughed. "Right in the *middle* of this party? Why would we want to do that?"

Aimee shook her head. "Because *I* want to get out of here!" she said. "*I'd* like to go home!"

"Go home? Why would anyone want to go home? This party is fantastic! Darnell and I were invited in by the kind host. The music is going strong. The ambience is wonderful. The drinks are solid. And despite all the shit you talk about them, these people are fine. I don't understand. What's the problem?" he asked.

"The problem? This place is crazy. Benjamin died, you fucking idiot! Right in front of us, and they did nothing!" Aimee exclaimed.

"Yeah, but the rest of this place is amazing!" Rod said.

"No, it's not! The damn stars are gone! Odessa is a fucking nut! And don't even get me started on that pervert Trevor!" Aimee said.

"They're not *that* bad," Rod said shrugging. "Back me up, Darnell!"

"I dunno, Rod," Darnell said uncomfortably. "She's not wrong. And I kind of want to leave too, now."

"Thank you, Darnell!" Aimee said. "At least one of you is sensible! I want to get the hell out of here."

"Aimee, you worry too much," Rod said. "Come with me, and we can get another round of drinks."

"I don't *want* another round of drinks," she said, giving Darnell an imploring look.

"I *want* you to take me to the door!" she said, looking back at Rod.

"Fine," Rod said. "But after that, I'm going back to party. This whole door thing you two have going is kind of a downer."

Rod led the trio with a drink in his hand as they walked out of the house.

"This way, this way, lady and gentleman," Rod said sarcastically as he led them down the front steps to the gaslit path. "Come right this way, to the infamous door in the hedgerow."

Rod and Darnell exited the house and retraced their original steps, with Aimee in tow, down the path across the front lawn.

"C'mon. It was this way," Rod said pointing down the main path.

The whole scene – the house behind them lit up against the night, the all-out bombast going on over at the pavilion, and the gaslit path winding off down the hill – it all washed over Darnell, and he felt a strange sense of déjà vu.

"Man," he said as he shook his head, "it feels like forever since we first came through here."

Aimee frowned and shot him a look.

"Are you sure this is the way?" Aimee asked.

"I think so," Rod said. "Right, Darnell?"

Darnell didn't answer, and Aimee shook her head in disappointment.

As they walked down the path, the house grew smaller behind them. Blooms of gaslight poured from the lampposts that dotted the path, and the distant sounds of the party were reassuring in their vitality.

"Why do we have to do this?" Rod asked childishly. "It's just a dumpy old path that goes back to the dumpy old door in the hedgerow and the woods and eventually back to our dumpy old lives." Rod kicked a pebble for effect as they walked.

"My life isn't dumpy," Aimee said. "I'd like to get back to it."

"I'd like that too," Darnell said.

"That's great, I guess. But I don't like my life very much at the moment." Rod sounded angry. "You two do whatever you want. I'm gonna stay and have fun."

"I've had enough 'fun'," Aimee said. "I've had enough of this place."

"Can we just get out of here?" Darnell asked.

"Whatever, man. Damn," Rod said as the three of them arrived at the smooth paving stones of the base of the path.

The large, well-manicured hedgerow rose up to greet them. But instead of a large wooden gate with a curiously twisted iron knocker, they were met by a large, uninterrupted swath of leaves and branches.

"What's going on?" Aimee asked. "Is this the place you were telling me about?"

Darnell looked at Rod. His friend looked back in confusion.

"It's not here?" Rod asked.

"It was right here," Darnell said, running his

fingers through the leaves of the hedge. "I swear it was right here. Right, Rod?"

"Guys, is this some kind of bad joke you're playing?" Aimee asked, her tone rising.

"This looks just like where we met David," Rod said.

"It *is* where we met David," Darnell said. He pointed at the bench. "He was sitting right there! In the dark, smoking a cigarette."

They looked at each other, their faces steeped in confusion and anxiety.

"Because if this is a joke, it isn't funny," she said, sounding wary.

"No, I swear this isn't a joke!" Darnell said earnestly. "The door. It was right here. I promise you!"

"Well, it's not here now!" she said.

"It was here. This is where we came in," Rod chimed in.

Aimee looked so angry that it seemed like she might cry.

"So either this door has disappeared, or you two are lying."

"We aren't lying!" they said in unison. Darnell looked hurt, Rod outraged.

"Just let me get this straight. You're both saying that there was a giant door here and that it disappeared?"

"Yes," Darnell and Rod said at the same time, but their voices were uncertain now.

She shook her head in exasperation. "Please forgive me if I don't believe you," Aimee said in a flat tone.

"What?" Darnell asked, affronted.

"Please forgive me if I don't care," Rod replied.

Aimee looked at him, tears welling in her eyes.
"Fuck you!" She yelled at Rod. "I'm going to see Raymond."

"I'm going too," Darnell said, backing her up.

"Maybe he can show us a way out of here," Aimee said.

"What do I care about a way out? This party is banging," Rod asked.

"Look asshole, you can come with me or not," Aimee said. "I don't care."

Aimee turned and made her way back up the gaslit path. Darnell gave Rod a withering look and ran off to follow Aimee.

Rod laughed, then reluctantly followed them both.

The Groundskeeper's Cabin

Darnell, Rod, and Aimee walked down the overgrown trail that wended its way through the trees and followed it to the groundskeeper's cabin.

The small, rundown cabin sat slumped in the middle of a dark clearing. A dim ruddy glow came from the windows. Darnell walked up to the cabin and peeked inside.

"There's a couple of dying embers smoldering in an old coal stove," he said to Aimee and Rod.

Rod shrugged, and Aimee gave him a flat look, so he knocked on the door. A few uncomfortable moments of silence later, Darnell knocked again.

"Maybe you should knock louder," Raymond's deep voice said from behind them.

Aimee and Darnell turned, startled.

Raymond emerged from the shadows in the woods behind the trio.

"Please. We need your help," Aimee said.

"I'd say," Raymond said.

"Why are you way out here? Hanging out in the woods?" Rod asked.

"I can't stand to be around those snobs," Raymond said, gesturing back up the path.

"What do you mean?" Rod asked. "That party is awesome."

"Rod, this party is not awesome," Aimee said. "A guy just died. So shut it." She turned to Raymond. "So why are you all the way out here?" Aimee asked.

"I'd just rather be alone," Raymond told her. "It's better that way."

"What were you doing in the upper floors when Benjamin died?" Aimee asked Raymond. "Just watching?"

"I was getting some air," Raymond said. "I visit the smoking den every now and again. Otherwise, I'd prefer to keep away from them."

"If you hate it so much, why don't you just go home?" Aimee asked. "Why stay all the way out here in the groundskeeper's cabin?"

Raymond looked serious for a moment.

"So you haven't realized yet?" he asked.

"Realized what?" Aimee asked anxiously.

"You won't be leaving. You can't."

"Have you tried?" Darnell asked.

Raymond laughed, "Of course."

"Like, really tried?" Darnell asked.

Instead of answering, Raymond took a deep breath and asked, "Ever noticed that you can't see the stars here? Or the moon?"

"Of course we have," Aimee answered, her anxiety rising. "What does that have to do with anything?"

"So you're stuck here? How long?" Darnell asked Raymond.

"A long ass time," Raymond replied quietly.

"You don't know how long?" Darnell said.

"Listen," Raymond said seriously, "David isn't what he seems. And this ..." He paused. "This party shit is only skin deep. You wouldn't believe the shit these people have done." His face twisted in disgust.

"It's all the more reason we have *got* to get the fuck out of this place," Aimee exclaimed.

"Don't worry too much," Raymond said to Aimee. "It's not so bad when you get used to it. The food and drinks never run out."

"See! And that's a reason to *stay!*" Rod blurted.

"No!" Aimee snapped at him. "That is *not* a reason to stay. That's a trap. We have to get out of this stupid place."

She turned to Raymond.

"Will you help us?" Aimee asked.

"I don't think I can," Raymond replied. "I just don't have it in me anymore."

"So it's like that? You've just given up?" She was furious. "That's just cowardly!"

Raymond winced.

"Why did you tell us to come out here if you couldn't help us?"

"I had to tell you!"

"Tell us what? To stay?"

"I thought knowing would help," Raymond replied. "What else do you want from me?"

"This is pointless," she exclaimed. "I thought you could show us a way out. All I want to do is leave."

"All you ever do is whine about leaving," Rod said to her. "I think this place is great! I want to stay here forever."

"I dunno, Rod," Darnell said. "I gotta back her up on this."

"I don't care if you back me up," Aimee said. "I'm going to find a way out of here with *or* without you."

She stormed off, stamping away from the cabin.

Darnell left the clearing to run off after her.

Rod was left alone with Raymond. He had no idea what to say, so he turned and walked slowly away.

Don't Come Any Closer

Aimee clutched her purse to her body and ran as fast as she could away from the cabin, through the woods, to the main house. Darnell stretched his legs and ran faster to make up for her head start. Eventually, she slowed down to a fast-paced walk.

"Why are you following me?" she asked, shooting a furious glance over her shoulder as they progressed down the overgrown path through the woods.

"I just want to help," he said.

Aimee set off running again and left Darnell behind as her feet pounded furiously down the path. They both ran flat out for a moment.

"Wait," he said, as he started to struggle for breath. "Wait up."

Aimee ignored him and kept running. She reached the back of the house and collapsed against the wall, crying, tears flowing freely down her cheeks.

"Hey," Darnell said, as he approached her.

"Don't 'hey' me," she said roughly. "I hate it when guys say 'hey' in a stupid, soft voice."

"I just want to help you!" Darnell said.

"Help? You know what would help?" she asked in a manic voice. "If you just *left me alone!*"

"Do you really believe that?" Darnell pleaded. "I think we need to stick together if we're going to have any real chance of getting out of here!" He took a tentative step forward. "Aimee?"

Click.

The cocking hammer of the gun sent a tremor of anxiety skittering down the back of his neck.

"Don't. Come. Any. Closer," she said firmly, her eyes red and puffy from crying. She pointed the pistol directly at his chest.

"Wait," he said in confusion. "That ... that was in my pocket!"

He patted his jacket pocket, where the gun should have been.

She nodded, sniffling. "I took it while we were dancing."

"Okay. Easy now," Darnell said.

She pointed the gun at his head. "Don't tell me what to do."

"Okay, but what did I do to deserve this?" he asked in a calm voice. His hands were raised high in the air.

"Because you lied to me!"

"We didn't li—"

"*Shut up!* I don't know you or Rod, and you *lied* about how you got here," Aimee interrupted him.

"Whatever that stupid little story you two made up was, some utter crap about coming through a fantastical doorway in a hedgerow."

"It wasn't crap!"

"I went through a door too!" She gestured with the gun. "I was just working late, running an experiment! The next thing I know, a doorway appeared! And it led to this stupid fucking *Twilight Zone* episode. This is such *bullshit*." She quivered with anger, the gun vibrating with her fury.

Darnell spoke in an even tone: "Look, we can find our way out of here, together."

"I don't need you," she said with fire in her eyes. "I needed your door because my door disappeared. Now I have no way home." She looked Darnell dead in the eyes.

"I don't ..." Darnell began.

"Just leave me alone, Darnell." She spoke in a dead voice.

"Wait," Darnell offered.

"Stay the fuck away from me," Aimee said as she turned away from Darnell. Placing Rod's confiscated pistol in her small black purse, she sprinted off into the darkness, leaving Darnell stunned and alone.

End Part One

Interlude

Raymond watched Rod as he disappeared into the woods, then turned and walked to the groundskeeper's cabin. He unlocked the heavy door, went inside, and slammed it shut behind him.

The cabin's walls were made of heavy beams with sandy mortar between them. Small glass windows adorned the front of the building, and a thick wood-shingled roof sat on top.

Inside, the light was dim, and the ceiling was low. The shadows were thick across the ground, like carpet. Off in the far corner, near the smoldering embers of a fire in a coal stove, Raymond Lawrence saw a shadowy version of himself sitting in a rickety wooden rocking chair.

The other version looked up with stern eyes glinting and said, "You know you ought to help those poor people."

Raymond winced visibly at hearing this articulated so clearly. "I know," he whispered. "But I can't."

"You mean, you won't. You won't get up off your ass to help these poor stranded people." He shook his head in obvious disgust. "You saw that woman. She's beside herself."

"There's nothing I can do!" Raymond cried to his other self.

"You can try at least. You can get out there and contribute."

"What can I do?" Raymond cried.

"Don't you still want to get out of here?" his other self asked.

"I tried to escape. It never worked ..."

"So you gave up?" his other self asked. "Go help them!"

"It's no use! I can't get them out of here!"

"Maybe you can't get them out of here. But you can help."

"I don't know how," he said quietly.

"What has this place done to you? When did you become so weak?"

Raymond let out an anguished sob.

"You know what to do," his other self said.

Raymond pushed open the door to the groundskeeper's cabin and went back out into the night. As he left the house, he looked over his shoulder – there was no trace of the other Raymond, only the empty cabin and the darkness left behind as the embers were extinguished.

David stepped through the narrow window on the fourth floor and out onto the highest balcony in Gilbreth Manor. He looked out below him and surveyed the raucous party that still raged on below. Some of the partygoers had fashioned a raft from lawn tables and had an umbrella as a sail. They charged forward toward the pool house to throw their boat into the pool, where it would immediately sink to the delight of all the drunken revelers. Lights twinkled in the distance, illuminating nothing but smiling faces, glistening red with inebriation.

He lifted his gaze from the pool house and scanned the back porch and the lawn. The band played steadily, and everything was moving along at its own chaotic pace. As he scanned the party, he caught a glimpse of Raymond Lawrence watching Aimee from the shadows as she ran away from the party.

David and Raymond locked eyes.

David's smile flattened out for a moment.

But only for a moment.

Part Two

Falling

Darnell opened his eyes.

He found himself sunk down deep in a comfortable crevasse cradled by the cushions of a large wingback chair. Checkered red-and-green patterns decorated the upholstery that framed him, shooting forward from either side. The night sky swelled around him, bright with pale moonlight and swathes of twinkling stars. The air was cool and tasted wet, like it would before an autumn rain. A breeze flowed, uninterrupted by any trees or buildings.

Darnell looked around, and everything in his field of vision seemed to stretch out before him, all of it just a little too wide, too long.

He looked down and saw David seated in the twin smoking chair across from him at a small, maplewood breakfast table. The table was perched on the peak of the highest roof of Gilbreth Manor, teetering over the estate and the property that sprawled out around it.

David was wearing a black suit with a pencil-thin necktie, and between them on the table, there was a white porcelain tea set embellished with red accents. "There's tea," he said, and poured Darnell a cup. David handed Darnell his teacup on a small saucer.

As Darnell accepted it with a shaking hand, the cup clinked in the saucer. "The stars are beautiful," Darnell mentioned.

David nodded as he sat back in his chair and sipped his tea.

"I feel like I haven't seen them in so long," Darnell remarked.

"We can't always see them, but they've been here with us all along," David said.

"Where is here?" Darnell asked. "Why can't we leave?"

David pointed to the sky.

A sense of dread washed over Darnell, and he looked over at the edge of the gray slate roof.

"No one is stopping you," David said in an ambiguous tone.

Darnell set his tea down. Then he found himself standing. His head felt light, and he turned and put his hand on the wingback chair for support. The whole world seemed so large, and the sky above him was endless.

The slate roof of the house was old, and the tiles were heavy, dusty, and slightly crumbling at the edges. His left foot took a step, and then his right foot. And then he was moving, as if in slow motion, toward the edge of the roof.

David smiled.

Step by inexorable step, Darnell's feet carried him forward. He desperately wanted to stop. But he couldn't and didn't know why.

He closed his eyes and took another step.

The edge of the roof was only a step away.

He squeezed his eyes shut like a child with soap in them and willed his body to stop walking.

Stop.

Walking.

He felt the blood rushing to his head as adrenaline pumped in his veins.

And then his body took that last step.

His right foot stepped off into empty space, followed by his left, along with the rest of him. His adrenaline-fueled wave of terror became a full-blown flood of incomprehensible emotion. His mind was awash with the acute despair that only the falling know.

He opened his eyes and immediately wished he hadn't.

The air whooshed in his ears as he watched the house pass swiftly by.

He closed them again, trying not to think about what he'd just seen.

The ground.

It was rushing up to meet him.

But just before they touched—

Darnell opened his eyes.

Or did he?

He couldn't tell. He was facedown on a floor somewhere, and the worn wooden floorboards smelled familiar. He stood up and found himself looking at a poster he recognized.

Darnell froze with his mouth agape.

He was in his old room. The room where he had grown up in his grandmother's house. He could smell her cooking from the kitchen. Since she died, the earthy, rich smells of her food were something he only experienced in dreams.

He walked slowly over to the door to his room. The old brass knob was dented and loose in its setting. He turned the knob. The hinges creaked as he opened the door.

He stepped through.

He found himself once again on the floor in the center of the room he just left. Confused but determined, he stood up again. The same poster stared at him. Jimi Hendrix stood sweating on a stage on the poster, playing a guitar cut into a curious, twisted shape, like the knocker on the door in the hedgerow.

He tried the door again.

He found himself on the floor again.

Jimi was still sweating.

His grandmother's cooking still smelled so delicious.

He stood up in the same room, looked at the same poster, and opened the same door. And ended up on the same floor.

Every time he crossed the threshold, he found himself on the floor again.

Frustrated, he began to run through the door over and over, repeating the same sequence, until he was so angry he could cry. He had no idea how he was supposed to exit this endless series of doorways, and the harder he tried, the more futile his actions seemed.

He cried out in despair and put his hand on the door again. Before turning the handle, he heard something.

A voice?

A woman's voice, very faint, coming from behind him.

"Wait!" the voice said, as if across a great distance. Darnell hesitated and pulled his hand back from the dented knob.

"Wait!" the voice said again, louder this time.

He turned around.

The room disappeared, and in its place was a pale gray field, stretching off into the distance.

In the center of it all stood a large wooden door.

The wooden door had a twisted iron knocker on it. It was shaped like Jimi's guitar on the poster, and like the knocker he'd seen on the door in the hedgerow.

The door opened, and an arm reached through.

"Come on!" Aimee's voice called. "This way!"

Darnell took one step and then another as he walked toward the door. He grasped the outstretched hand, and its fingers tightened around his and pulled him through.

Penny for Your Thoughts

Aimee was alone.

Far away from the crush of the main party, she had found a little trail paved with smooth stone. It led in the opposite direction of the pavilion and the music that emanated from the outdoor band. It was cut into the far side of the hill from the house and ended in a small, circular park with a beautiful marble fountain in the center surrounded by brick paving stones.

Old maple trees lined the edges of the park, their branches outstretched. The landscape was lit as though there was a full moon, but she could not see it in the sky.

Aimee saw a small girl balanced on the fountain's ornate rim, placing one foot delicately in front of the other, walking the perimeter of the fountain.

The girl's hair was long and black. She wore a small, shin-length, white dress, with little poofs of silk at the shoulders. On her feet were little red shoes with shiny buckles. An ornate diamond brooch was pinned to her chest – it sparkled in the night, its strangely twisted shape gleaming brightly as light reflected from its surface.

The girl moved gracefully, and Aimee couldn't help but notice that she looked so terribly alone, doing her little balancing act all by herself. The girl saw her coming and regarded her coolly with large, dark eyes as Aimee walked up the path but didn't stop her movements. Then she went back to concentrating on her feet.

"Hi," Aimee said quietly as she neared the fountain.

The little girl glanced at her again and sighed.

"Why do you look so sad?" Aimee asked.

"Because it's my birthday," the little girl said, "and my family is awful."

"You're Penny?" Aimee asked in surprise.

Penny nodded in silence. She corrected her balance and continued to traverse the perimeter of the marble fountain.

"I'm Aimee. Happy birthday, I guess?" Aimee wished her lamely.

"It's not really that happy," Penny said in a sullen tone and gave her a guarded look. "I hate it here."

"Right. This place creeps me out too," Aimee said nervously.

Penny shrugged again and said nothing.

Aimee laughed awkwardly and looked up at the dark and starless sky.

"It's weird you can't see the stars here," Aimee said

to change the subject.

Penny didn't respond right away. "Mom said this party was for me, but it sure doesn't feel like it," she said eventually. "I hate her," Penny said of her mother. "She doesn't care what happens to me."

"I don't like my mom much either," Aimee said.

"Your mother is nothing like my mother," Penny said. "My mother is evil."

Aimee didn't answer.

"I don't matter to her at all," Penny said. "This party is more for her and her friends like Trevor. Like David."

"David?" Aimee asked. "I didn't realize this party had anything to do with him."

"It doesn't matter. My mother won't say anything about it. She just keeps going on and on about all the amazing people in attendance. And how much she loves me. It's all lies."

"I'm sorry, Penny," Aimee said. "That's terrible."

Penny shrugged delicately.

"I hope it was worth it for them, I guess," Penny said. "I don't mind the party, really. I just avoid them all. It's easy."

Aimee looked down and kept her silence.

"It's okay. At least you're here now," Penny said and smiled.

"For now at least," Aimee said seriously.

Penny smiled and skipped around the marble fountain, looking a little happier than she had before.

"For however long you stay, then," Penny said happily. "We can be fast friends."

"I'm glad you want me here, Penny. But I can't stay here with you forever," Aimee said.

Penny laughed aloud. "Oh Aimee, you're so funny. I like you." She smiled. "We'll be such close friends," she said.

Aimee just smiled uncomfortably as Penny came over and hugged her. Aimee hugged her back but did so hesitantly.

"Here, take this," Penny said, reaching into her dress pocket. She pulled out a delicate silver chain, on the end of which dangled a spindly silver key.

"I don't understand," Aimee said. "What is this?"

"You'll figure it out," Penny said.

"Figure what out?" Aimee asked, looking down as she fastened the silver chain about her neck, and dropped the key down into the front of her dress. There was no response, and when she looked up, the little girl was gone.

The Twin Smoking Chairs

Rod was alone.

"I want a drink. Like, yesterday," Rod said to the trees as he walked back to the house.

He meandered up the dark path past the overgrown part to its intersection with the gaslit path. He followed that to the back of the manor and went in through the back door near the pool house.

Once inside, he went directly to the bar in the main hall, its pyramid of liquor rising like a beacon above the crowd. He cut through the rivers of people that wandered up and down the dais steps that led to the bar, looked up at the gigantic painting of Odessa's naked body standing behind it, and smirked.

People on the dance floor clapped their hands and moved their feet to the music of the band. The twin grand staircases flared out of the first floor and curved up to the second floor like wings above the party.

"A whiskey, neat." Rod ordered a drink. He

downed it, and his hands stopped trembling.

"Two more and I'll feel even better," Rod said to the bartender.

Rod nodded his head and tapped his feet to the band's feverish antics for a moment while he enjoyed his whiskey. He wandered away from the crowd congregating at the main bar. Every maneuver through the party involved a negotiation between duchesses and lords, vapid sports stars, and wildly dressed women – he made it to the stairway and up the curve of one of the grand staircases to the second floor.

He continued over the marble tiles of the landing to a large, ornate door with a placard on its face that read, "The Office of Percy Gilbreth."

He turned the brass knob, pushed the heavy wooden door, and with a slight squeal, it swung in. Rod walked down a short hallway, past a small, half-sized door to his left, and out into an expansive study.

He peered around the room.

There was a fireplace with a fire burning in it and a large wooden desk with burnished gold accents and a leather office chair behind it. The ceiling was high and dark, and its ancient beams were cold and cobwebby. Any space outside of the work area on the desk was piled with papers, and the room was dotted with teetering towers of documents.

Checkered red-and-green patterns decorated the large wingback chairs in front of the fire. Over the side of the chair to the right dangled a careless hand, swishing a glass of whiskey. The hand disappeared for a moment, then fell back to its original position.

A strong smell of wood and cigar smoke enveloped him.

"Is that you, my lucky Penny? Have you come to see me? Has your party been wonderful?" A low voice came from the chair.

"Uh, no." Rod cleared his throat. "My name is Rodney. Hey, isn't the smoking room around here somewhere?"

"Oh," the voice said, deflated, "I thought you were my dear Penny. Do come in though. Pour yourself a scotch and sit with me for a moment." The voice slurred as it spoke. "I haven't had a proper guest in such a long time. A long, long time."

Rod poured himself a glass from the crystal decanter on the nearby stand and walked toward the fire. Moving closer, he began to see around the large wingback chair.

"I'm Dr. Percy Gilbreth, by the way," the man said.

"Yeah, I saw your name on the door," Rod replied.

Percy was a large man, gray and bald, with gold spectacles. He was dressed in a tuxedo as most of the male partygoers were, but it was rumpled. He was slumped in the chair, hardly moving but for his hand ferrying the glass to and from his lips.

He never looked away from the fire, and his grayish eyes looked as if they were staring into the distance, even as Rod knocked over a tower of unmailed letters on his way to the vacant wingback.

"Sorry," Rod apologized.

"Don't mind it a bit," Percy said absentmindedly. He still hadn't looked up.

"Should I pick these up?" Rod asked.

"Leave it, my boy, and tell me, what's your story, Rodney? I haven't seen you around. What is it that you do?" Percy had a slight New England accent, and his words were drawn out.

Rod sat down in the empty wingback.

The big chairs were comfortable, and the patterned fabric cradled Rod and Percy as they sat by the fireplace, the only warm section in the whole cold room. The scotch was smooth and warm in the dusty atmosphere of Percy's office.

"I'm an actor," Rod said, and slouched lazily in the cushions of the chair.

"Really? An actor?" Percy asked. "That's fantastic! I love the stage!"

Rod gave him a strange look. "You don't mind if I smoke?" Rod asked.

"Oh, a cigarette? I would love one. Here, here. Let me get you one, my boy," Percy placed his glass on a nearby table, reached into the large, ornate humidor next to it, and fished out two brown cigarettes.

"Here, take this blunt instead. You seem like you could use the pick-me-up," Rod said, handing the old man a short cigar roll.

"Thank you, dear boy," Percy's eyes lit up. "That's very kind."

"No, thank you, Mr. P for all your wonderful hospitality," Rod said in an elaborately polite manner.

"We'll save these for later," Percy said as he touched the box of expensive cigarettes and smiled. He picked up a large table lighter, lit the cannabis-filled cigar, and took a drag.

Then a second.

And a third.

Then, after a slight pause, his breath caught in his throat, and he coughed. A cloud of bluish swirls moved toward the fireplace, then dissipated.

"Curious herbs you have here, Rodney. Where did you get them?" He continued to smoke with a thoughtful look on his face.

"Yeah, I rolled this earlier. I got it in Schenectady," Rod said and pulled out his own joint when he realized Percy wasn't going to pass the cigar back to him. He lit it with the marble table lighter.

"So, I've got to ask. Why are you just sitting up here and not enjoying your party?" Rod asked, coughing.

"Don't worry about me, dear chap," Percy replied, staring off into the fire again. His face grew serious once more. "I just need some time … away, you know? To think."

He put the blunt out as you would a cigar and lifted his glass of whiskey.

"I get it," Rod said, drinking his drink. "Believe me, I do."

Percy muttered noncommittally in response as he took another sip of his drink, lost deep in some distant memory. He inhaled like he wanted to say something and then exhaled slowly before speaking. "Have you ever done something you regret, Rodney?" he asked. "Something unforgivable?"

Rod paused, taken slightly aback.

Percy continued. "You may not think this just to

look at me, but I have done terrible things, Rodney my boy. Do you know such shame that you remove yourself from the world, separate yourself from everything for so long that you begin to ask yourself if you still exist and why?"

"Not really," Rod replied. "That sounds awful."

"Not to worry. It's nothing more than I deserve." Percy lapsed into silence for a moment, and they both drank more of their scotch.

"Some people say this old house is haunted, though I've yet to see a ghost," Percy laughed suddenly. "The only ghouls I've met are some of the people I'm closest to."

"I met your wife down there," Rod replied. "She *is* quite the lady."

"Odessa? She's all glamor and no go. If you know what I mean," Percy replied, sipping his whiskey.

"I don't," Rod said, doing the same.

Percy didn't respond.

"What about Trevor?" Rod inquired.

"That hack? He's nothing. Merely hired to translate the book for us. A rank amateur that got a little too cozy with Odessa. Now she believes his occult bullshit. He served his purpose, though," Percy said hatefully. "Don't get any ideas. She's crazy, you know."

"I rarely get ideas," Rod replied. "About anything really."

"Probably the best approach, I must admit," Percy said. "I've lived my life having all sorts of ideas about all sorts of things, and look where it got me."

Rod looked around, "I don't know. It looks like

you're doing pretty well to me."

"It may look that way to the untrained eye, I'll admit," Percy said. "But all that glitters is not always gold, my boy."

"You are so right, Mr. P," Rod said.

Percy's eyes glittered coldly in the flickering light of the fire. The shadows climbed up the walls behind them. Percy handed Rod one of the cigarettes he'd fetched earlier.

"I think I'm going to clear out," Rod said to Percy. "Thanks for the scotch."

"It's been delightful, my boy," Percy said as Rod took the cigarette. "Do tell Penny to come visit if you see her."

Rod nodded and held on to the cigarette.

"I will," he promised. "And thanks."

"Of course, dear boy," Percy replied amicably. "Come back anytime."

Rod nodded appreciatively, lit the cigarette, and walked out.

"Poor guy," he said to himself after the door closed. "He really needs to get out sometime."

Rod took a drag from his cigarette as he walked across the tiled marble landing and down the main stairs to the first floor.

Darnell

D arnell opened his eyes.

He was in the passenger seat of his grand-mother's large sedan, feeling as if he was riding on a cloud as low brick houses and the occasional church or grocery store passed them by. The car was built like a tank, of leather, glass, wood and old, heavy plastic. His grandmother was sitting in the driver's seat, hands at precisely ten and two on the wheel as she maneuvered the large sedan down the street from his school.

As the sun glinted off the chrome of her old American automobile, Darnell knew he should feel safe, but he didn't. Green lawns and freshly painted cars drifted by outside the window.

"How was school, honey?" Her voice was gentle but her words muffled, as though they were coming from far away.

The world was bright and green, and the road

signs were hot in the sun. They flowed past Darnell in a blur.

"Honey?" she said. "Can you hear me?"

Her voice was slow and thick, like molasses. He supposed he answered her.

He was looking up at her and at the blue sky behind her beautiful face. She smiled at him and nodded, gazing out down the long hood of the sedan. Everything looked perfect in this bright little world, but Darnell felt an overwhelming sense of dread.

His grandmother slid her long, graceful fingers across the hard steering wheel as they merged onto the interstate. She pointed the barge-like car down the road and glanced at him as she accelerated. She smiled, and it was beautiful.

He noticed her fingers grip the steering wheel a little tighter.

Her steering grew erratic, and her eyes began to look strained.

He felt the long sedan shift direction.

"I ... feel a little peculiar, baby," she said. "I might need to stop for a bit."

She jerked the car back to the right, and he felt the smooth pavement cross under them and then the roughness of the tires driving onto the shoulder of the road. Gravel peppered the underbody of the car as she pulled to a stop.

"Don't worry, honey," she said as she put it in park. "I've got you. You're safe now," she said, and winced in pain, lurching forward against the steering wheel, eyes practically bursting from her sockets.

Darnell felt his voice vibrate in his head as he cried out.

He lurched toward her.

His hands touched her shoulder as she hunched over, convulsing.

Aimee's hand reached into the car through the passenger's door.

"You don't need to see this again," she said, and pulled him out into the light.

©

Darnell opened his eyes.

The day was clement, and the birds chirped in the trees as he trudged down a rocky path with mountains spread out wide before him in majestic splendor. Everything about the day would have been nice if it hadn't been for the weight of the boulder he was carrying across his shoulders. It was a giant thing, rocky and dense, that began to crush Darnell as he advanced over the rough terrain, sweating under the load of it.

It seemed to grow heavier with every step.

Everything else around him, from the wildlife to the trees, seemed carefree and easygoing. If only he could get rid of this stupid boulder and stop it from crushing him beneath its weight.

Every step he took down the flower-lined path made him more frustrated.

The harder he struggled to hold the boulder up on his shoulders, the harder it weighed down on his neck. It pressed and pressed down on him until his face was sagging down toward the dirt path.

The bones in his legs and back buckled, and as he fell, the boulder crushed him. The enormous weight of it pressed his face into the dirt, and he closed his eyes in pain.

He accepted his fate and stopped struggling against the weight of it.

Once he'd given in, he abruptly found himself standing near the boulder unharmed.

But then it wasn't a boulder at all.

Now that he had accepted it for what it was, the once unmanageable boulder had become a ball that rolled easily. He began his walk down the scenic mountain path again, and the ball rolled smoothly down the path alongside him, requiring very little effort from him, just a bit of maintenance now and then.

He rolled it along with him as he crossed the mountainous terrain, over rises and through valleys, and continued on his way.

He ran and ran, and time passed.

And the ball stayed beside him.

A smile came to his face. His speed increased as he ran ever faster.

He closed his eyes.

The dream shifted.

Darnell opened his eyes.

He was standing on the front lawn of Gilbreth

Manor, looking up at the house on the hill, silhouetted against the night sky. Large floor-to-ceiling windows on one of the upper floors glinted in the night.

He felt a pressure looming at his back, a low roaring wind that swelled into a menacing presence behind him.

Darnell scrambled away from it and began to run toward the house.

He ran up the gaslit path, his feet pounding, first on the dirt and then the painted wooden steps that led up to the porch. He sprinted in through the front door as the roaring darkness closed in behind him.

Darnell burst into the deserted foyer and ran through the main hall. The house was empty as a tomb.

The roaring darkness swirled through the doorways and windows, filling in the space behind him. Vague forms could be seen glinting in the inky black, just below the surface.

He sprinted up to the third floor as the darkness clawed at his heels, dragging him down by his arms, roaring louder and louder. He turned to face the darkness as its growling reached a crescendo but continued to stumble backward and fell through a doorway as he watched the inky cloud almost envelop him.

The door closed.

He was in a room with floor-to-ceiling windows and shadows all around.

The darkness had been cut off by the door closing; it roared and snarled in anger as it beat against the barrier. The room seemed insulated from the whipping darkness, despite the wild noise coming from outside. He turned around, and there, to the right-hand side of the room was a vague group of shadowy figures, encircling an altar.

Floating above them, a great red, curiously twisted rune glowed in the darkness.

He walked right up to it, parting the crowd of indistinct figures. He placed both palms upon the glowing, bloodred face of the rune, his eyes wide, reflecting the twisted red shape.

The rune obliterated all other thought, and then consumed him.

PJP, the Deuce

Rod was led away from the party by Odessa toward the huge private zoo behind the house. He tried to walk and take a sip of his cocktail at the same time and failed. Odessa laughed at him as he spilled his drink and pulled him along by his tie.

They strolled out past the pool house to the complex of cages and pens that sprawled out on the grounds behind the main residence.

"Where are we going?" Rod asked Odessa drunkenly as she led him to the entrance of the zoo, which was down the hill from the pool house, tucked away in the dark woodlands that surrounded the outer property.

At the entrance was a large wooden stable. Rows and rows of horses slept in the stalls, whickering and snoring as Rod and Odessa walked by.

"I knew you'd want to spend some time alone with me, Rodney my dear," Odessa said.

"Oh did you?" Rod laughed, playing coy.

"Oh yes," she said in a low voice. "I could see it in your eyes. The very moment we met."

Rod gave her a cartoonish wink.

They looked at each other for a moment, their faces flushed from booze. She patted his hand affectionately and sighed into the pause as she led him past the wooden fenced pens for llamas and zebras.

"I'm so tired of the men in my life," she volunteered in a flat, careless tone as they walked. "They bore me to tears. I can't stand to listen to their voices." She pursed her lips. "You on the other hand, are new," she said. "And very pretty."

"That's true. I am very good looking," Rod said without a hint of irony.

Odessa rolled her eyes. "And vain too. So vain." She laughed. "But you're comfortable with yourself, and that's more than most people can say. Not like the rest of the bores back there and their tiring conversation."

She twirled her fingers into his as she walked him past the large grassy space for the elephants, the large, four-legged gray shapes moving slowly in the darkness, raising their trunks to strip leaves from planted trees' branches to munch on.

"Really? How can you be tired of this place?" Rod asked in disbelief, looking at the lumbering shapes moving slowly. "I love it here."

"I can tell." She arched an eyebrow. "It's written all over your face." She smiled a feline smile. "I just want to compliment you," she said. "But it's difficult to do with that stupid look."

"I love compliments," Rod said.

Odessa smiled a wide and possessive smile. "You're so beautiful and stupid." She shook her head. "I love that I can tell you anything and that you won't understand a word of it."

"Oh, I can do *that* for you, sexy lady. I promise," Rod said cheerfully.

She laughed a deep and sultry laugh, and gave him a look through her lashes as she led him past the monkey enclosure, where a small plot of land was caged in with a single large tree in the center covered in sleeping monkeys, who were draped over the branches and snoring away in the darkness.

"My husband is a frightened little man who never leaves his office, except to go to his laboratory every once in a blue moon to look at his stupid, broken machine." Odessa looked over the caged monkeys with a scathing expression. "And Trevor, while good looking, is such an insufferable, unimaginative boor. They're both so useless I could scream. Between you and me, I was the only one who ever had any vision."

"I mean, you do have great eyes," Rod said.

"Shut up. I was the one who got us here, you beautiful fool. Who got us everything. No thanks to any of them, their friends, or my bratty little daughter," she complained as she led him away from the monkeys and on further into the zoo. "Ungrateful, the whole lot of them."

"You have such an amazing body. Nobody would ever know you've had a kid," Rod said.

"Thank you, Rodney," she warmed up. "This is why I'm glad you found me again. I'm tired of dealing with whimpering cowards. I've met everyone inside that place, and none of them excite me anymore. They're all minnows in a fish bowl. You're a shark. You say what you want and look good doing it. I like that."

"I wish everyone thought that way," Rod said.

"They don't?"

"Not the studio execs that fired me. Not my greasy creditors, trying to squeeze me for every nickel I'm worth."

"Mmm. You sound angry, dear," she said, her voice heating up. "Your voice gets so deep. I love it."

Odessa smiled at him as they passed a big brick pen that housed furry black bears, all balled up and snoozing under a large, man-made rock shelf.

"I am angry, dammit! And I should be!" His voice rose with each word, and Odessa's smile widened at his anger. "But you know what? Fuck those guys. Fuck all of them and what they think. Fuck my stupid creditors! I've made it this far!"

One of the bears closest to them rolled over and eyed Rod grumpily, but it was a sleepy gesture, and it closed its eyes immediately afterward.

"Who's going to stop me now?" Rod asked with a triumphant smile.

"With a face like yours? No one. I bet people give you the world," she said with a wink. "Look at how handsome you are."

"I know, right? I'm handsome as fuck, and I appreciate you for noticing that, Odessa." Rod said, as

he looked around at the bear pens. He turned to her.
"What the heck is all this? Where are we?"

"Percy's zoo," Odessa said. "Once upon a time, he used it for his studies. Now I frequently use it to hide from those morons. Come, let me show you."

"This must have cost a fortune," Rod looked around at all of the cages and pens and brick enclosures that housed Percy's animal collection. Odessa led him toward a large, caged enclosure beyond the bears' pen.

"It's all because of Percy and his obsessions," Odessa said in a wry voice.

"He says the animals 'help him with his practice.' He 'keeps them for research purposes,' 'for their scientific value,'" she said, "but it's all rather dull if you ask me."

"Mm-hmm. 'Research purposes,'" he said flatly. "'Scientific value.' I bet I could show you something of 'scientific value.'"

"Oh yes?" she asked in a husky voice as she looked down at the front of his trousers.

"Oh yes," he said in his smoothest voice. "Let me show you."

She looked back at him through lowered lashes and ran her fingers through his hair.

"You may be annoying, but I can't resist that face," Odessa said. "Don't worry about a thing. You come with me."

She looked satisfied, like a cat that had killed a mouse.

"Haven't you realized?" Rod asked. "We'll both

come together, you sexy beast."

"You'll have to prove that to me," Odessa chuckled as she sauntered off between the animal cages.

"Where are you going, woman?" He asked in a faux-stern tone.

"You'll see," she said in a low voice and crooked her finger at him, beckoning. "I want to show you my favorite animal."

"Grrr," Rod growled flirtatiously, making clawing motions with his hands.

She just smiled and led him to a large, caged grass-and-brick area with ominously high wire fences surrounding it.

"What are these giant fences for?" Rod asked.

Odessa laughed at him in delight.

"I love big cats," she said as she traipsed down the path. "I love the way they move. And I love my Leopold most of all."

She gestured to the pen before them before she turned and leaned back against the high fence, shooting Rod a lustful look. A large white Bengal tiger lay sleeping in the grass, black-and-white stripes rippling in the night air.

"Oh, do you?" Rod replied as he walked up. He stood over her and wrapped his fingers around the bars of the cage behind her.

They locked gazes.

"I like the way *you* move."

"You're such a charmer. Those eyes of yours," she looked up at him.

"They make you look like a big cat," she said, her

pupils dilated.

"A big cat, eh?" Rod asked, his fingers slipping beneath the straps of her dress, slowly moving them aside.

"Will you let me eat you up?" he whispered.

She pulled him closer to her by his lapel and kissed him.

"Shut up," she said between movements of their lips. They kissed for a long moment, and then Rod flipped her around with a firm grip, and she gasped. He grasped her from behind, running his hands up the front of her dress to grab her breasts as she faced the bars of the animal enclosure.

Odessa gripped the bars of the cage tightly. She pushed her back into him and felt the bulge in his pants pressed against her. She reached back and up over her head and grasped his ears with a low, soft chuckle and then gasped as he lifted up her dress.

She moaned in pleasure as Rod entered her from behind and gave a low and guttural animal grunt. Across the grassy space behind the bars, Leopold raised his huge head from his paws where he lay. The tiger's yellow eyes blinked lazily as it looked at them.

"Oh, Leopold is watching us!" Odessa exclaimed staring at Leopold's giant observing eyes as he licked his lips with his rough pink tongue.

Rod thrust his hips against Odessa's.

"*Oh!*" she exclaimed.

"So what?" he asked. "I used to own a tiger. They couldn't give a shit about humans fucking. I did it a million times in front of him. He always looked bored out of his mind."

"Are you kidding?" she asked.

The tiger grew more interested in them as they moved with more enthusiasm.

"No way. Pope John Paul II was awesome," he said, thrusting his hips, pushing hard inside her.

"Who cares? Just fuck me!"

"We just called him Deuce for short," Rod's attention wandered, and his actions became slightly mechanical.

"And then he bit my intern," he said, out of breath, slowing between thrusts but still increasing the intensity of each one. "One day, Deucy just flipped while we were on set. There was a tuna sandwich."

"Who cares about—*oh*—your tiger's tuna sandwich?"

"Not the tiger, stupid. The intern. They thought it was because of the tuna sandwich she had, but nobody really knows."

"Don't call me stupi—oh!" Odessa burst out.

Rod thrust his hips even harder, burying himself in her.

"Shut up," he said, sweat beading on his forehead. "Let me finish … my story. She was just bringing me my skinny latte and then *bam*." He thrust as he said "bam." "He bit the shit out of her. And so they canned me from my own damn show." He pounded at Odessa with redoubled intensity. "And somehow I ended up here!"

He pushed her roughly up against the bars of the cage, and the tiger looked at them with more interest as the noise of their encounter increased.

"Oh!" Odessa said.

"And now she's gonna sue my balls off," Rod said between thrusts. "Like there's gonna be anything left after these creditors finish selling off my whole life. And all because I told the intern to get me tuna for lunch."

Leopold was pacing up near the fence now, letting out short roars. Each roar caused Odessa to moan louder, as her face flushed with blood. As the tiger circled closer and closer, the pitch and volume of Odessa's voice rose.

Rod escalated his efforts, his face growing beet red.

Then, all of a sudden, his voice rose up to a crescendo, drowning out Odessa's moans. Before she was able to get any satisfaction, he cut off abruptly and let out a deep sighing moan as he climaxed, falling forward on Odessa's back, spent.

There was an icy pause, and Odessa's back was rigid.

"You all done back there, champ?" She asked in dry contempt.

"Oh, for sure," he said in a dreamy, satisfied tone as he pushed himself off of Odessa.

Red Flags

Darnell opened his eyes. He was alone in the dark.

He could feel that he was slumped in a corner with his legs jammed against the adjacent wall. He reached out and felt a door.

He winced and touched his head, bathed in darkness, then grabbed his stomach.

The back of his head was throbbing, and it smelled like he was in a musty closet. He brushed his fingers across the large knot on the back of his smooth, shaved scalp and winced in pain as he came in contact with the sore spot.

He reached out gingerly and groped about with his hands, slowly feeling his way around the painted plaster walls of the closet that surrounded him. He groaned softly in pain.

"I heard noises coming from in there." Darnell heard a muffled voice say through the wall. "I think he's awake."

"So what if he's awake?" said a second, deeper voice.

"What do we do?" the first voice whispered.

"We wait! Like Trevor told us to do," the second voice said with scorn.

"But—"

"But nothing. Just sit still. The boss'll be here any minute."

"Fine," the first voice said sullenly.

Through the wall, Darnell could hear footsteps nearing.

Then the door to the closet opened. All Darnell could see at first were blooms of light dancing in front of him, then a tall man's shadowy form emerged.

"Get up," Trevor said.

Darnell's vision started to clear. He could see Trevor before him, holding an absurdly large golden candelabra, its flames casting shadows across his face from below. Trevor glared at him with perfect brown eyes, his slim-fitting three-piece suit looked rumpled, his black jacket unbuttoned, his fine black leather shoes scuffed. Darnell could see nothing of the room beyond the door.

"Stand him up," Trevor said to the two densely muscled men in cocktail attire who were dawdling outside the door.

The two gruff-looking men snatched Darnell up from the floor of the closet, each one gripping him by a bicep while he groaned in pain and discomfort. Once he was upright, he slumped between them, unable to stand on his own.

"What's with the stupid candelabra?" Darnell mumbled groggily. "One candle wasn't enough?"

"Shut up, you," Trevor said. "I'm the one asking the questions."

"That was a statement," Darnell mumbled. "I'm the only one who's asked a question so far."

"Stand him up," Trevor commanded his two goons.

Darnell groaned as the two men stood him up straight.

Trevor leaned in until his eyes were level with Darnell's, and he brought the candelabra up beside their faces so it illuminated both of their eyes brightly.

"Where is she?" Trevor asked in a sneering voice.

"Who?" Darnell asked slowly.

"Aimee, you mouth-breathing fool. Tell me where she is!" Trevor's dark-brown eyes were twinkling with malevolence.

"I don't know. I ..." Darnell's head was pounding. "I lost her."

"Where?"

"I can't remember," Darnell answered honestly. "I was following her, and then she was almost back to the house."

"And then what?"

"Then I felt a terrible pain," Darnell replied. "And everything went black."

Trevor turned from Darnell to the two men. "He was following her!" Trevor shouted angrily, accusing the first, taller man and then the shorter, squatter one.

"She was right there, and you decided to take him? How did you lose her when they were both right next to each other?"

"We didn't see her!" the shorter, barrel-chested man whined. "He was alone when we picked him up."

"Unbelievable," Trevor muttered. His pretty face twisted angrily before he moved closer to Darnell. The two men holding his biceps clamped their grips down even tighter.

"Don't think we aren't watching you," he warned. "Whatever it is you think you're doing ..."

"Dude, what is your problem?" Darnell asked. "You've been an asshole since we first got here."

Trevor barked a laugh.

"No, you're the asshole," Trevor said. "This place is a paradise, and you wanna mess that up."

"I think 'paradise' is a little strong, Trevor," Darnell replied. "Besides, we're not trying to ruin anything. We just want to leave."

Trevor got so close to his face that Darnell could smell the sweet rot of his breath. The flames from the candelabra licked at Darnell's chin.

"Leave?" he sneered as a wide-eyed Darnell tried to pull away from the flames, but Trevor's two goons held him still in their vise-like grip. "We're going to make you wish you'd never come here," Trevor said coldly.

Darnell gave him a sharp look of fear.

Then they all heard a creak at the door.

"Who's there?" Trevor called out, holding the candelabra toward the door as he peered into the darkness. Darnell sighed in relief as the flames were taken away from his face.

For a moment, there was silence. Then the door flew open.

"Trevor, what are you doing in here, tormenting this poor guest?" Fiona asked from the doorway, her green eyes, flame-red hair, and red dress muted in the shadows.

"None of your business," Trevor said defensively. The two bodyguards pushed in front of him, standing between him and Fiona.

She laughed. "You need all this protection against little old me, Trevor? You really are such a coward. And everyone knows you'd rather be playing with Aimee than Darnell here," she said with a smirk. "Why don't you go torture her and leave Darnell with me?"

"Tell me where she is, and we have a deal, Fiona," Trevor said.

"She's out by the fountain," Fiona said. "Talking to Penny."

"Penny?" Trevor asked loudly. A concerned expression flitted across his face, then he turned to his two lackeys. "Let's go!" Trevor said in a petulant voice as he stormed off through the open door with his bodyguards following behind.

"I can't stand that guy," Fiona said to Darnell.

"I thought he was gonna kill me."

"Oh, don't worry about that now," she said as she stepped closer to him on quick, light feet, covering the distance from the door to where Darnell stood near the closet in an eyeblink.

She stepped abruptly up on the tips of her toes and tried to kiss him.

"Oh really. No," Darnell pushed her back instinctively.

Her dainty frame tumbled backwards, but she easily recovered her balance.

"You really are beautiful," Darnell said. "But I'm so stressed out, I can't even think about sex right now. I just want to find my friends and get out of here."

Fiona squinted her emerald-green eyes as she thought for a moment. "I know where your friend is," Fiona said. "I can take you to him."

"Oh yeah?" Darnell asked hopefully. "How do I know I can trust you?"

"You can't," she said with a red, glossy smile. She grasped his hand and led him away from the closet, around the dusty, cloth-covered table that sat in the center of the old disused dining room.

"What is this?" Darnell asked, as Fiona turned a light fixture on the wall.

In front of Darnell, a door-shaped piece of wall moved toward him with a click and slid to the side.

"It's my private little room," Fiona said, pointing into the chamber. "Now go."

"In there?" Darnell asked, alarmed. "I would really rather not."

The fair-skinned twin turned to him with a pile of white powder in her open palm. Before Darnell could react she blew on the powder, and a cloud of it enveloped his face.

"Rod's not in here. Is that coca—" Darnell lost

the will to speak halfway through his sentence, as he breathed the powder in.

"Stand on one leg," she commanded him.

Darnell found himself standing on one leg. His eyes fluttered violently.

"Very good. You're learning now, aren't you, Darnell? My sister and I always get what we want," she said. "Go inside," she barked.

Darnell's body stepped through the door and into the purple, windowless room. There was a small bed on one side, chains hanging from the headboard. The bed was wide enough for two people and strewn with messy purple sheets. Suits of armor lined the back wall of the room, each one painted the same purple as the walls.

Fiona followed Darnell in and closed the door behind them softly. Then she walked to the bed, sat on it, and crossed her legs.

"Stop. Stand there and face me," she pointed to a spot on the floor directly in front of where she sat. Darnell moved automatically to where she pointed and turned to face her.

His eyes were wide as he looked at her in fear. Sweat rolled down his brow, and veins throbbed in his temples.

"Do a little strip tease for me, won't you," she said.

Darnell let out an anguished moan through clenched teeth as he struggled to stop himself from complying.

Fire flashed in her eyes. "Don't fight the drug. Do it!"

Darnell's body sprung into action, swaying as if to unheard music. He kept his anguished eyes locked on Fiona. One fat tear rolled down his cheek as he moved against his will.

He let his designer blazer slip from his arms and hit the floor.

Then he unlaced his tie and tossed it to the ground as well.

His fingers deftly unbuttoned his shirt against his will and then unzipped his pants to reveal purple-and-gray striped briefs beneath.

"Stop," she said seductively. "What nicely colored underwear."

The curly hair of Darnell's chest could be seen through the opening in his half unbuttoned shirt.

"Continue," she said.

Darnell's hands pushed his pants down, and they fell to the floor, fully revealing his underpants, with a bulge beneath them warping the purple-and-gray-striped pattern.

"And you said you couldn't even think about sex," she said looking at his crotch. She leaned forward, and sensuously ran her hand up the inside of her leg as she pulled the red fabric of her dress back to reveal a delicate tuft of flame red hair.

"Get on your knees. I want you to eat me," she commanded as she leaned back on the bed and spread her legs wide.

Darnell's body stepped over his discarded shirt and pants as he got down on his knees. His eyes rolled around in horror as his body leaned in between Fiona's legs and pressed his tongue between her fire-red lips.

"Ah!" she exclaimed in pleasure, and wrapped her alabaster legs around Darnell's bald head, locking him in. She rubbed the top of his head with her hands as she moaned.

"Don't stop, you bastard!" She growled in pleasure and bucked and writhed as she clamped her legs down around Darnell's head. His face oscillated faster and more furiously as he matched the rhythm of her escalating moans.

Then Fiona screamed, convulsing around Darnell, crushing his head with her thighs, and digging her fingernails into his ears. She arched her back into an almost impossible position as she went rigid in furious climax.

She made Darnell keep going for a little while longer as she spasmed and laughed in pleasure before putting a hand on his forehead and pushing him away.

"Stop it," she commanded. "Go over there." She pointed to a bare spot on the floor near the bed.

Darnell inhaled a massive gasp of air when he was finally allowed to detach his mouth from Fiona's crotch. Tears rolled freely from his eyes now, as he stood up. His lips twitched, but he was still unable to speak.

Fiona just lay there laughing at him. She glanced at his hands as his fingers started to quiver.

"So my little concoction is wearing off, eh?" Fiona asked, looking slightly miffed. "Let's get you tied up before you can fight back."

"Get on the bed," she said, as she stood up, and pulled her dress back around her legs to cover her pubic region. "Lie on your back."

Darnell's body moved to comply, but it was jerkily resistant now. He kept his tear-filled gaze locked on her emerald-green irises as he tried to beg her to stop, his lips twitching more violently.

He sat down on the bed, and then maneuvered himself into the center of the mattress.

Fiona giggled as she reached for the chains that hung from wrought iron loops in the bed's headboard, and clasped the shackles around his wrists. Then she grabbed the chains that ran through the other iron loop mounted at the foot of the bed and shackled his legs.

"S … stop," Darnell finally managed to croak out, the veins in his neck bulged as he strained to utter the words.

"But why? You don't seem to be hating this," she said, running her hand up Darnell's leg to linger on the bulge in his striped underpants. She reached down behind his head and leaned in like she was going to give him a kiss.

Darnell squirmed and tried to angle his face away from hers.

Fiona stopped short, her lips next to his. "Let's see if there's anything else you like, you filthy man," Fiona said, as she reached her slim white hand beneath the pillow and pulled an ornate automatic pistol from behind Darnell's head.

"Ah!" Darnell moaned, and fresh tears leaked from

his eyes.

"You keep making all this noise," Fiona said. "But your body betrays you. All you men are the same."

Fiona pressed the point of the pistol into the throbbing bulge in Darnell's cotton briefs and grinned as she ran the cold metal sensuously over his skin.

She climbed onto the bed and straddled Darnell, draping her dress over him, hiding the point where her soft flesh rested against his thin underwear. She brought the point of the gun to her lips. Her sharp tongue flitted out, touching the tip of the barrel.

Darnell's eyes widened in fear.

"Don't be afraid. It's hardly loaded," Fiona said with a sharp laugh, pointing the pistol at Darnell's chest, tracing lines around his nipples with the cold metal of the gun muzzle.

Darnell whimpered and squirmed and tried to scream.

"Do you want to find out?" Fiona asked Darnell as she held the gun with both hands, pointing it straight-armed at his nose.

Darnell shook his head. "N … No!" He managed to croak.

"Let's see," Fiona said, and cocked the hammer. Darnell let out a pitiful whimper, and just before she pulled the trigger, she aimed it up at the ceiling.

Bang!

Darnell wailed through half paralyzed lips.

Fiona looked at the gun in surprise. "Huh, I guess it *was* loaded," Fiona said, hefting the pistol. "Feels light." She pointed the gun back at Darnell's face, right between his eyes.

Darnell was so exhausted, all he could do was sigh deeply. He stared down the barrel of the big .45 and then looked into Fiona's green eyes.

"Maybe I underestimated you," Fiona said. She pressed the gun into Darnell's forehead.

He never took his eyes off hers.

Her finger tensed on the trigger.

At that moment, the door to the purple room slammed open, and David appeared.

"Was that a gunshot?" he asked. "I thought I heard a gunshot."

"You came just in time to watch," Fiona said to David with a wicked smile, pressing the barrel into Darnell's sweating flesh.

She pulled the trigger.

Click.

The hammer clicked down, but no bullet came out.

Darnell made a tiny whimper and went limp. "Save me," he mumbled, covered in sweat, staring at David.

"I'm not sure poor Darnell here is enjoying himself, Fiona, dear," David said. "Maybe you should let him up."

"You're such a downer," Fiona accused him in a sulky tone as she slid off Darnell. "Darnell and I were bonding."

David walked over to the bed. "You've bonded quite enough for now," he said. "Give it here."

He held out his hand, and Fiona passed the gun

to him with a dirty look.

David began to untie Darnell from his restraints as Fiona collected her things, grinning as she left the purple room.

Old-World Vice

"Penny?" Aimee asked, standing on the paved-brick walkway that encircled the marble fountain as she scanned the circular park, but the place was deserted. "Penny?"

"Penny's not here," Trevor said from behind her.

"Ah!" Aimee yelled in surprise as she turned around with a startled jump. "You again? Why are you lurking out here in the dark?"

Trevor and his two goons stood in the darkness on the grass beyond the paved brick.

"There's no one here to help you now," Trevor said as they closed in on her.

Trevor's two muscle-bound bodyguards grabbed Aimee by her shoulders and dragged her away from the fountain onto the grass.

"This is for making me look stupid in front of everyone," Trevor said to her as he began unbuckling his belt with a toxic grin. His two sneering friends manhandled her away from the fountain.

"Hold her down," Trevor commanded.

"No!" Aimee screamed. "No!"

Trevor's two muscular guards pushed Aimee down on her back in the cold grass. She twisted against their hands as she thrashed and bucked, attempting to maneuver her body in some way that might break their iron grip.

"Get. The. Fuck. Off. Of. Me!" she screamed again.

One of her wild kicks caught the right goon in the legs, and his grip on her faltered. In that split second, she managed to break free from the grip of the other man and scramble away from them as she ran back toward the fountain.

"Don't let her get away!" Trevor whined, hastily buckling his belt. "She's making you look like fools!"

Trevor's two sycophants began moving toward Aimee.

Aimee struggled to run through the grass in her high heels as she made her way back to the fountain with grass clinging to her hair. Frantically, she jammed her hand into her small black purse, fumbling for the pistol inside. She could hear the three men moving up behind her as she managed to get her sweaty fingers around the pistol's grip.

She reached the laid brick path that encircled the fountain, then turned around, widened her stance, and aimed the gun at the three men chasing her, her hands shaking. All three men put their hands up and paused. But a greasy smile remained on Trevor's face.

"Stay back!" Aimee said, cocking the gun.

Trevor continued inching closer to her with his hands up, smirking while taking slow step after slow step. Eventually he stood right in front of her, leering.

"Get back, you gross motherfucker! I hate you," Aimee said, gesticulating with the gun.

"You love it," Trevor said. "You know you do."

He managed to get so close that Aimee was pressing the gun into his chest. Her hands were shaking.

He laughed. "I knew it," he said. "You can't do it."

Aimee's finger trembled as she started to pull the trigger.

He moved suddenly and batted the gun from her hand before she could fire. It flew in a slow, heavy arc into the fountain, hitting the water with a loud splash and sinking swiftly beneath the surface.

She screamed in anguish as Trevor sneered at her.

"If you aren't going to give it to me, no one can have it," he said. "Get her." Trevor snapped his fingers at his brawny followers.

The two men grinned salaciously at her, and closed in on her from both sides. They clamped down on her, one man grabbing her bicep, and the other crushing her shoulder with his huge hand.

She kicked and cursed them as they dragged her to the fountain.

"I love watching you struggle," Trevor said, grabbing a hunk of hair on the back of her head and muscling her toward the water.

"Let me go, you sick fuck!" Aimee groaned as she struggled at the fountain's lip.

Trevor pushed her face toward the surface of the

water, the corded muscles in his forearms hardening as they tensed. Aimee put her hands on the coping of the fountain and pushed back against Trevor, her muscles writhing as she resisted.

She could see her horrified reflection in the water and, behind that, the wide and twisted smile on Trevor's face.

"Don't fight it," Trevor said in a slimy tone. "This place was never for you."

She pushed as hard as she could against the marble fountain's rim, sweating with the effort of trying to resist Trevor's weight. The veins in her neck throbbed as he pushed her head inexorably closer to the water.

"No!" she screamed.

Trevor leaned harder on her, tightened his grip on her hair, and forced her head further down, grunting from the exertion.

Aimee's face was red, and she uttered a guttural sound as she almost reached the water's surface.

Trevor laughed as he leaned against the back of her head with all his weight.

The tip of her nose broke the surface tension of the water, making a ripple where it touched.

Trevor leaned down and flicked her ear with his tongue as he laughed softly and forced her down. "You deserve this," he whispered maniacally.

"St—" she said, her voice interrupted by water entering her mouth.

Then she heard the deep voice of Raymond commanding Trevor: "Let her go."

All of a sudden, the pressure on the back of Aimee's head disappeared.

She stood up, coughing, water dripping from her mouth, and looked.

Behind her, Raymond had tackled Trevor into the grass and was raining blows down onto his face, as Trevor struggled to escape from beneath Raymond's bulk.

Trevor's two goons ran over and prised them apart, kicking Raymond in the process. Raymond stood up quickly and raised his fist to his chest in a single motion, making it clear he was grimly ready for a fight. One of Trevor's men cocked his arm back and aimed a blow at Raymond, who easily dodged it. While the assailant's footing was unsure Raymond punched the man twice in the head. With a spray of red blood and a confused look, the man fell on all fours away from Raymond.

The remaining guard swung at Raymond, who again dodged the strike. He threw an answering punch, but the man blocked it with a raised forearm. Then Raymond grabbed the man's arm, pushed it down, and headbutted him viciously.

He pushed the injured man to the side and walked toward Trevor. The two muscle-bound men were sprawled, dazed, and injured on the ground.

"Why are you even here?" Trevor snarled at Raymond as he wiped the blood from his lips.

"I'm here to fuck you up," Raymond said as he exploded forward.

Trevor's eyes widened in surprise as Raymond tackled him.

Raymond's shoulder collided with Trevor's midsection, and he wrapped his arms around Trevor in a bear hug, lifting him from the ground with the power of his legs. He carried Trevor a little way down the hill toward the woods before slamming him onto his back in the thick grass. A loud grunt exploded from Trevor's lips. Trevor lay on his back, shielding his face with his hands, crying like a wounded animal as Raymond pummeled him.

The two stocky men struggled to their feet and ran back toward the brawl. They reached into the fray to stop Raymond's falling fists.

"Good riddance," Aimee said in a shaky voice as she dried her mouth, standing alone at the fountain.

The fighting continued to move further away from her downhill. In the quiet, she walked across the brick paving stones that surrounded the marble fountain. When she reached the far side of the fountain, she fished her cell phone from her small black purse and powered it up, her hands still shaking.

The screen lit up, but the display showed no reception.

Still no signal.

"Ah fuck, what do I have to *do* to get out of this crazy place?" she whispered to herself.

Aimee powered her phone back off and tucked it away again in her purse. She breathed deeply, catching her breath.

She looked up at the giant hulk that was Gilbreth Manor. Light spilled out of all the first- and second-floor windows of the house, illuminating the yard and trees and people all around it. The upper floors were dark.

She studied the house for a while longer, listening to the music and the people's revelry. Just as she was about to look away, she noticed a white flash of light glinting from inside the enormous floor-to-ceiling windows on the third floor.

She reached into the front of her black dress and pulled the spindly silver key out, cradling it in her hand. She looked back at the house, but the glint of light was gone. She took a deep breath and sighed before stuffing the key back into the front of her dress.

With a grim look on her face, she began to walk reluctantly back toward the house.

Unexpected Camaraderie

"Thanks for helping me out back there," Darnell said as he and David stood on the second-floor landing, overlooking the party below. David said nothing but smiled and nodded as he scanned the dancing crowd on the first floor.

The main bar was a hive of movement, as the bartenders served endless lines of partygoers, and the pyramid of liquor bottles behind the bar cast its amber glow onto the gatherers' faces, the giant painting of naked Odessa looming large behind it all.

Darnell put his hands on the bannister and turned to David. "Can you help me get out of here?" Darnell asked.

"What is here?" David asked. "'Here' is often relative."

"I'm just trying to get back to my rental cabin," Darnell said.

"I know you want to leave," David said. "But I

188

can't help you."

"But if you can't help me, who can?"

"No one, I'm afraid," David said. "That I know of."

"Come on. It can't be impossible. What do I have to do to get you to let me out of here?"

David said nothing.

"Is it a money thing?" Darnell begged. "Because I have money."

"It's not up to me," David said. "I am merely the host."

Darnell winced with a throb of pain. He raised a hand to rub the spot on the back of his head tenderly.

"Fucking Trevor. His stupid goons bashed my head in, and now it's killing me," Darnell said.

"I can help you with that," David said, reaching up and touching Darnell's forehead with his fingertips. Behind his closed eyes Darnell saw a burst of white light and his pain was gone.

Darnell took a long look at the man that stood in front of him.

David was coolly collected in his impeccable black suit, his thin black tie perfectly placed under his tie clip. His wave of black hair was still neatly oiled down, his ageless face unperturbed. He gazed at Darnell with eyes of some dark, indistinguishable color.

"What are you?" Darnell asked.

David looked at him curiously for a moment or two, then began. "I come from a distant place. And I can never go back."

Darnell just stared at him.

"So ... what happened?" Darnell asked, not knowing what to say.

"I changed, Darnell. I found out that I just want to party."

Darnell stood there looking confused.

"Don't worry so much," David said. "I encourage you to enjoy the party around you."

"I can't enjoy the party," Darnell exclaimed. "I'm fed up with this place! This whole night has been a fucking mess."

"How so?" David asked.

"I met up with an old friend, went on a bender with him, and everything has spiralled out of control since. This place has fucking traumatized me."

"I wish I could do more for you," David said.

"All I need is to find Aimee and Rod and get the hell out of here," Darnell said.

"I wish you luck," said David. He smiled and strolled down one of the mirrored main staircases into the bedlam below, leaving Darnell standing by himself, alone on the grandiose landing, overlooking the freewheeling chaos of the main hall. He turned and looked across the landing from where he stood.

There was a comically large door directly in front of him, larger than all the rest on this floor. So he walked over to it.

A brass plaque mounted on it read, "The Office of Percy Gilbreth."

He grasped the large brass knocker and slammed it down, knocking on the door.

Cat's Cradle

In the clearing outside the tiger cage, Rod and Odessa got dressed. Rod pulled his pants up and buttoned them. Odessa looked at Rod coldly as she smoothed her dress down over her thighs.

"I must say, it seems reckless to let your tiger bite someone," Odessa said. "Can you not control him?"

Rod gave Odessa a confused look as he zipped up his pants. "He's a tiger," he replied. "I didn't really 'let' him do anything."

"Don't make excuses," Odessa said. "It sounds like you trained your tiger poorly."

"Oh, fuck off. You think I need this right now?" he asked, straightening out his collar. "The thing was a wild beast. That's like trying to keep my lawyer outta my cocaine."

"Come come, Rodney. You know you enjoyed dominating that wild beast. Bending it to your will," she said.

"Uh, you might be projecting a little," Rod said, shaking out his sleeves, straightening them. "I don't think I *actually* dominated anything. He still bit the shit out of—"

"You know what would be really sexy?" Odessa cut him off in a husky voice.

"What?" he asked, centering the buckle of his belt.

Rod looked up at her. She leaned seductively against the bars of the cage, pushing her breasts up out of her velvet gray dress until her nipples crested the fabric. Her firm, toned skin gleamed in the night.

Leopold paced in the cage behind her.

"Come here," she commanded. "And I'll tell you."

Rod floated toward her as if drawn in by a string.

As he got close and leaned toward her lips for a kiss, she smiled and curled her fingers in his hair.

"I want to see you be a man," she said in a low, sexy voice.

"I can't help but be a man," Rod said confidently. "I'm just that manly."

In one swift motion, she unbolted the door to the cage and used Rod's weight as he leaned against it, pushing him inside the cage with the tiger.

Leopold stared at Rod with gleaming golden eyes and licked his lips with his wide, flat tongue that curled all the way up to his nose. The tiger paced closer, its muscles rippling under its sleek fur.

He growled at Rod, squared his shoulders and hunched down. Then the six-hundred-pound, striped predator pounced. The big cat flew through the air as Rodney desperately scrambled away down the side of the cage, trying to dodge the cat's long hooked claws.

Rod backed himself up against the right wall of the cage, his eyes wild as he kept his frantic gaze locked on the pacing tiger that growled near the door.

Rod heard Odessa cackling with glee as the tiger moved closer.

"Do you think he's trained not to bite, Rodney?" she asked, her eyes glittering feverishly.

"You're crazy!" Rod cried. "I knew it from the moment I saw your crazy fucking eyes. I knew you were trouble the moment I realized I wanted to fuck you." He grasped at the iron bars that surrounded him, futilely trying to climb up the side of the cage.

"Be a man, Rodney. Or are you just a boring little child, like the rest of the men in my life?" she egged him on.

"Why are you so cheerful? This isn't funny!" Rod said as he jumped and grabbed at the bars of the enclosure, only to slide back to the ground.

"Oh, you sound upset," Odessa said with a wicked grin. "Are you going to cry?"

"Maybe! If you don't get me out of here!" Rod yelled angrily in a panicked voice as he leapt up and tried to grab hold of the top of the cage.

Odessa grinned even wider as Rod gave up trying to reach the top and turned back to Leopold, who growled loudly.

"You sound so manly when you scold me," Odessa said, undulating herself against the bars with increasing fervor. "Do you like it when I misbehave?"

"No! You're being fucking awful right now!" Rod

cried as he skirted the edge of the cage, circling away from Leopold while keeping a sharp eye on him.

Odessa ran one of her long legs up and down the bars, tilted her head back, dangled her blonde bob wig, and laughed maniacally.

"Do you really want to get out of there?" she asked as Leopold approached Rod.

"Yes!" Rod said, the pitch of his voice rising as he hunkered in the back corner of the cage.

"Then I want to hear you beg for it." She cackled.

"Please, Odessa! Please, please let me out," Rod cried abjectly as the large, white tiger padded closer to him.

Leopold lunged.

"I don't want to die," Rod wailed pitifully, as he dodged, jumping out of the corner, and just managing to evade a swipe of Leopold's thick paw.

"Then beg some more," Odessa laughed maniacally. "You've disappointed me severely, so redeem yourself."

"Please, Odessa! Please," Rod cried, his voice cracking.

Rod ran in a half circle around Leopold, who crouched down in the center of the cage.

"Please, pretty please let me out. I'm *begging* you," Rod pleaded as he wedged his face in between the bars of the cage next to where Odessa stood.

"Don't get stuck, darling." Odessa laughed nonchalantly and flicked Rod on the nose. "He'll eat you like a little snack."

Leopold bunched the muscles in his legs and

shoulders, tensing like a compressed spring.

"Let me go," Rod's voice fractured, as he bordered on tears. "I'm too beautiful to die!"

"You're such a baby," Odessa said, flicking the door to the cage open with a single, elegant finger. "I never locked the door."

"What?" Rod howled in an anguished mixture of frustration, astonishment, and hope. He glanced over his shoulder just as Leopold leapt. Rod dove toward the open cage door with Leopold only inches from his back, long teeth gleaming and wicked claws outstretched.

Percy and the Machine

Darnell stood outside Dr. Gilbreth's office, the large door looming in front of him, and reached up to use the brass knocker. The knocker bounced off its strike plate as Darnell knocked. For a while, no sound came from behind the door.

He knocked again.

Still nothing happened.

He pressed his hands against the wood of the door, hung his head, and closed his eyes.

"No one is coming," Darnell said to himself in despair. "I'm going to be stuck in this stupid place forever."

As he slumped against the door, his head in his hands, he heard a faint sound through the wood as something stirred behind it.

Darnell raised his hand to knock again, but before he could, the door opened with a slight squeal, and

Percy peeked out.

"Oh!" Percy exclaimed. "You startled me, good fellow."

"Sorry!" Darnell said, putting his hand down. "Who are you?"

"Says right here on the door."

Percy pointed to the brass plaque with his name on it.

"Are you going to come in? Or just sit there on my doorstep?" he asked, sounding like a kindly old grandfather.

Darnell straightened himself up.

"What's your name?" Percy asked.

"Darnell," he replied as he entered Percy's office.

"Come along, Darnell," Percy said and patted Darnell on the shoulder. "You caught me in the middle of something."

Darnell walked through the door into a short hallway, registering the small, half-sized door to his left that Rod had seen.

Beyond the hallway, he could see Percy's study, with its lonely burning fireplace, high dark ceilings, its stacks of papers teetering on every surface, and the twin smoking chairs that faced the fireplace.

Percy closed the door to his office behind Darnell. "I was about to go check on my machine upstairs when I heard you knocking." Percy turned and opened the small door in the wall. "Come," Percy said and ducked through the door into a narrow staircase beyond. "Follow me."

"Upstairs?" Darnell asked.

"But of course," Percy said.

"Wait, I remember now," Darnell said. "They say you never leave your office."

"That's not quite true," Percy replied. "Sometimes, I just want to go up to my workshop and look over this baffling computational device of mine."

"Computational device?" Darnell asked. "What? Like a computer?"

"I've never heard anyone use that word in a conversation before. Dear fellow, you must know more than you let on. Come, come. Let me show you the source of my problem," Percy said in an excited voice.

"Um, okay," Darnell said, following Percy through the tiny door.

The stairway he found himself on was far steeper than a normal one, narrow and climbing. A single pipe ran along the length of the entire thing and served as a crude handrail. They went up, past a switchback, and then up again.

"Is this it?" Darnell said, slightly out of breath.

"Not this door," Percy said. "One more flight."

Percy led him up past another switchback to a door at the very top of the staircase. The final landing was dark and hotter than the rest of the house. It smelled like an old attic. Percy slid the small door into the wall and stepped through.

He turned the lights on, and racks hanging from the ceiling powered on, row after row of light bulbs coming to life in sequence, accompanied by a series of loud electrical cracks. Before them were rows of shelves lined with jars that contained the preserved corpses of ancient, wrinkled animals in formaldehyde.

"What are these?" Darnell asked, looking at a particularly ancient rodent floating in a jar.

"These are unimportant," Percy said. "Just a record of my many failures. Follow me. The machine is this way."

"Is this a cat?" Darnell asked.

"That was Odessa's first cat. Leopold I. He lived much longer than usual but was in such terrible pain at the end that the experiment could hardly be called a success."

Percy shuffled off between the high shelves of jars.

"Come on," he said to Darnell over his shoulder, his pale-blue eyes twinkling.

Darnell looked away from the prune-like shapes in the jars and followed Percy. Beyond the shelves, the two came out into an open, sprawling workshop. Closest to the jar-lined shelves was what looked to be a medical lab, with an operating table, lights, and all manner of surgical instruments scattered about on clinical white tables.

The other side of the workshop was a large, well-equipped machine shop with tools mounted on hooks in the walls and milling and machining apparatuses scattering the edges of the room.

In the center of the workshop, there was an enormous machine.

The giant mechanical device sat at the center of it all, a massive, analog contraption rife with springs and triggers, all stacked in tall columns and spreading out to the widest point near the base.

"My masterpiece, and my folly," Percy said grand-ly.

The machine was large, and smelled of oil. It was ten feet tall and contained within a brass frame. A series of half wheels and inner joined gears were held in repeating patterns in the machine's innards, each one decorated with elaborate engravings.

Percy walked up to the machine. The wall behind him was lined with electronic equipment filled with readouts and dials.

"What does it do?" Darnell asked in amazement.

"Well," Percy said sadly, "it's supposed to do some-thing. But it was never completed."

Percy grasped a large handlebar protruding from the side of the machine, the clockwork interior mov-ing as he cranked. He ratcheted it forward a notch or two, and checked the settings against a formula he had tattooed on the underside of his left forearm. The machine's parts moved together seamlessly, a dance of mechanical perfection.

"And how far from complete is it?" Darnell asked.

"It's very close to complete. Klara, my lead engi-neer, said the designs were incredibly advanced for their age. What you see is what she built from the schematics, but we were unable to complete the last piece due to its complexity."

"Can the machine work without the missing piece?"

"You'll see when we activate the power."

Percy turned from where he was standing and flipped a series of switches on the wall behind him, then grasped a giant handle and put all his effort into tripping the gigantic switch. The racks of suspended electric ceiling lights flickered and dimmed as the machine powered on. The readouts and dials of the large, old electronic equipment lining the wall behind him began to light up, needles jumping in their housing with the surging electricity.

Lightning arced and climbed between the metal rods of the machine. Teeth meshed with teeth, timing the gears, and a million pieces joined together in perfect harmony.

"This is the most beautifully engineered thing I've ever seen," Darnell exclaimed.

"Isn't it," Percy shouted over the noise of it all.

The machine chugged along, making its infernal racket for a few moments more, building up to a frenzied crescendo. Then, after all the noise and drama, it just wound down with a forlorn sound.

"What happened?" Darnell asked, slightly disappointed.

"If I knew, it would work," Percy said. "This infernal machine is one of the sources of torment in my life; Trevor and my wife are another; and Penny, well ... that's a story for another time."

"Penny?" Darnell asked.

Percy shook his head sadly.

"I did something unforgivable to her and have been living with it ever since," Percy said.

"Ever since what?" Darnell asked.

"That's not your burden to bear," Percy replied in a sad, hollow voice, pointing to a workbench that was littered with copies of designs and plans.

"This is all we have of the design, all my transcribers could copy from the book," he said. "Even though I have endless time, I'm afraid I don't have the right mind to comprehend them. I am a doctor of biology, after all."

Darnell leafed through the blueprints, admiring the craftsmanship and intricacy of the ancient designs.

"What do you make of it?" Percy asked Darnell.

"This is really complex, Percy," Darnell replied. "I don't think I can help you with it."

"Pity."

"But, I think I know someone who might be able to help."

"Oh really?"

"She's a scientist, so she would definitely know better than I do."

"Well, what are you waiting for, dear fellow? Go get her!" Percy exclaimed, and ushered Darnell toward the exit.

Leopold's Folly

Darnell left Percy's office and was shutting the large door behind him when Rod came running around the corner at the distant end of the hallway, his face drained of color.

"My *God*, man, am I glad I found you!" Rod blurted as he ran up to Darnell, with his clothes dishevelled, his hair messy, and a wild look in his eyes. "I can't even explain! That lady was *crazy!*"

"What the heck happened to you?" Darnell asked in a startled voice.

"What happened to me? Some *real shit* just happened to me! This insane woman just locked me in a cage with a fucking tiger, Darnell! I barely survived!"

"A tiger?" Darnell asked in a small voice as he looked over Rod's shoulder.

"Yeah, man, a big white tiger!" Rod panted.

"A *white* tiger, you say?" Darnell asked.

"Yeah, a big stupid stripey white tiger named

Leopo—"

"*That tiger?*" Darnell pointed over Rod's shoulder, his eyes wide with fear.

Leopold loped down the hallway, his magnificent white-and-black-striped fur rippling, and his shining great eyes trained on Rod and Darnell.

"Help!" Darnell turned back to the office door and tried to open it. But it was locked, so instead, he began knocking desperately on it.

"Mr. P! Open the door!" Rod cried, as he beat on the door along with Darnell.

"Don't let that thing near me," Percy wailed from behind the door, his voice muffled. "I *hate* that stupid tiger!"

Leopold stalked toward them.

"Run, Rod, now," Darnell said in a breathless rush.

They sprinted away from Percy's office, across the second-floor landing, toward the stairs to the first floor. Leopold bounded after them, gradually closing the distance.

"This is kind of exciting, huh?" Rod huffed as they ran.

"Exciting?" Darnell could barely speak. "What the fuck?"

They ran down one of the mirrored main staircases, bounding down the steps. Leopold's heavy paws struggled to get traction on the slick marble tiles of the second-floor landing. Darnell and Rod bounded down two steps at a time as Leopold skidded to a stop near the balcony's edge. The tiger roared and put his front two paws on the balustrade, gazing out over the chaos of the party on the main floor below.

The dancing.

The drinking.

The noise of it all was deafening, and Leopold licked his nose, apparently unsure whether or not to follow them down the steps into the melee.

Rod and Darnell ran toward a knot of partygoers that had gathered at the sparkling pyramid of liquor at the main bar, the giant painting of naked Odessa towering behind it.

"Did we lose it?" Darnell asked, as he looked over his shoulder.

"I ... think ... so." Rod huffed and puffed as he looked back. "I don't see him behind us."

But then ...

They heard a roar from above.

Rod, Darnell, and all the partygoers looked up and gasped collectively.

Leopold was glaring right at them from the second floor with his front paws on the railing of the balcony.

The tiger leapt up onto the wide banister, with his back legs primed to push him over the edge.

"Dude, no way," Rod said in disbelief.

And then Leopold leapt out into space over the party below.

Everyone screamed.

The six-hundred-pound tiger flew like an arrow off the second-floor landing. He stretched out full length and sailed through the air with his muscles rippling.

But the tiger had miscalculated his leap, and his rear legs collided with the back of the giant painting of Odessa, tearing through it as he fell. He crashed into the giant pyramid of liquor that backed the bar, and just like that, the party's centerpiece began to tumble down – shattering bottles which cascaded onto the floor around the partygoers in a rain of glass and alcohol and bits of painting.

The band stopped playing music, shocked expressions on their faces.

Rod looked at Darnell, his eyes bright. "Can we stay here forever?"

"You're insane," Darnell said as they tried to slip away from the chaos. "That tiger wants to kill us. Let's get the fuck out of here."

"Where's the gun?" Rod asked. "Let's shoot this thing."

"Aimee has it."

"What? How'd she get it?"

"I don't know," Darnell said, as he moved behind a gaggle of confused partygoers. "She took it sometime when we were dancing."

"Should've just let me keep it."

Darnell and Rod couldn't see the tiger, but a crowd of partygoers pressed together and gathered around the area where Leopold landed.

"Oh no," a woman gasped.

"Odessa is going to be *so* angry," a man's voice said.

"Why did the fucking music stop again?" another voice asked.

Darnell looked at Rod seriously. "We need to find

a way out of here, Rod," Darnell said. "I feel like I'm at some hellish casino where there's no clocks. How long have we even been here?"

"Who cares? It's an open bar! My cocaine bag is never empty. Darnell, dude. We crossed the threshold and ended up in paradise," Rod finished grandly. "You're talking about clocks!"

Rod and Darnell circled around the crowd of partygoers that were gawking at the wreckage of Leopold and the bar, and crept toward the main staircase opposite to the one they ran down earlier.

"Look at this shit! This doesn't seem like paradise to me," Darnell said and gestured around angrily.

Rod held out a speck of white powder on the tip of a golden rod. "Want a bump?" he asked Darnell.

Darnell slapped Rod's offer away, the cocaine scattering. "No, I don't want a fucking bump!"

Rod rolled his eyes.

Odessa suddenly appeared at the bar, looking imperious and angry, and the crowd parted around her in silence. Trevor trailed behind her with a sly look on his face. As the crowd parted, Darnell and Rod saw Leopold laid out in a pile of broken glass on the steps of the dais to the main bar. The giant tiger was unconscious and bleeding, and his back legs jutted out at a terrible angle, clearly broken. A veritable river of bright-red blood was running down the wide steps to the bar.

"Get this fucking animal out of here," Odessa screamed.

Several partygoers nearest Odessa crowded around

the tiger, their hands grasping, trying to find purchase in his reddened fur. They began to drag the limp form down the bar steps and across the floor of the main hall.

"Oh god," Rod whimpered, and hid his face in his hands. "It's her. We have to get out of here."

"What? Her?" Darnell asked. "Come on, don't worry about her."

"Those idiots are here somewhere. I know it!" Odessa yelled and stamped her foot. "I told them to *never* interrupt my party!" Veins throbbed in Odessa's temple, and her face was scarlet red.

"Did you hear her? Man, I *told* you," Rod whined under his breath. "She's fucking *crazy*."

"Get it together," Darnell whispered urgently.

He grabbed Rod by the sleeve, and pulled him along, continuing around the back edge of the crowd. The partygoers were getting restless, angrily calling for the music to restart.

"Find them!" Odessa screamed at the confused people around the bar.

Darnell and Rod made a wide semicircle to avoid them.

"Rod, there is a distinct possibility we might die here," Darnell said. "And I just have to get some shit off my chest."

"What? Now?" Rod asked.

"Yes, now. You need to grow up, Rodney," Darnell said seriously. "I'm trying to tell you this as your friend. You need to stop it with the drugs!"

Darnell shook his head.

"You need to get your shit together and help get us out of this mess you dragged me into."

"I didn't drag you into anything," Rod replied. "It's not like I forced you to come here."

They continued to move toward the staircase as the crowd milled around looking at each other.

"Okay, you're right," Darnell said. "But you're not doing anything to help. All you've done is fuck off and ask me to give you money."

"Because I need money!"

"Because you're selfish. I can admit my mistakes, Rod. Can you?"

"But I really *do* need money," Rod said. "My creditors really *are* going to kill me, and I didn't know if you'd care!"

"Well, yeah," Darnell agreed. "Now you know, and it all could've been so much easier if you hadn't been a dick."

"Well, fuck, Darnell. I'm sorry," Rod said.

They had reached the foot of the grand staircase, and Darnell put his hand on the marble railing.

Odessa was throwing a tantrum in the middle of the crowd at the bar. "One of them is tall and handsome with a stupid expression, and his friend is a black man!" she yelled.

Darnell turned to look at Odessa as he put his right foot on the first step of the main staircase. All the nearest partygoers turned their gazes on him and Rod.

"He's over here!" A voice called.

"Get him!" Another one said.

Darnell locked eyes with Odessa over the slavering crowd.

Odessa pointed at them.

Darnell and Rod turned to run.

"Surround them," Odessa said. "Keep them there for me."

The partygoers surrounded Rod and Darnell, keeping them from going any further up the stairway, and closed into a circle around them.

"Can I be honest with you?" Rod asked, as the circle of partygoers strengthened, people filling in behind the first row. Rod and Darnell stood back to back as they faced the angry ring of people.

"You think we're going to die?" Darnell asked.

"Sure is starting to look like it," Rod said. "Point is, I just wanted to say I'm sorry for being an asshole and taking you for granted."

"Look, it's fine. And about the money," Darnell said. "I can help you if we get out of here. All you had to do was ask, like a real friend."

"Really? Dude ..." Rod said, choking up.

"C'mon, dude, don't cry about it," Darnell said. "We gotta find Aimee and get the fuck out of here."

As Odessa strode through the crowd toward them, the circle of partygoers parted before her, and Trevor followed behind.

"Hey!" Aimee yelled from the top of the stairs. "You two dimwits!"

Darnell and Rod looked up at her.

The crowd of partygoers looked up at Aimee, and then back to Odessa.

"Run!" Aimee yelled at Rod and Darnell, walking down the stairway toward them.

Darnell and Rod tried to push through the angry mesh of partygoers and escape up the stairs; the furious mob snarled and howled, determined to bar their path. They frantically wriggled and scrambled to find a gap in the web of arms and legs that blocked their escape.

Darnell leaned his entire weight against the boundary of the tightening circle to force his way further up the stairs.

"Help. Me," Darnell said to Rod in a strained voice. "Push me."

Rod piled his weight behind Darnell and heaved.

The ring of partygoers surrounding them finally broke, and Darnell popped out, followed by Rod. Up the stairs they ran, with Trevor and Odessa following closely behind.

They ran up to Aimee, who was standing halfway up the stairs, and then past her.

She stood her ground.

They turned and looked behind them in confusion and surprise, just in time to see Trevor running up to her, ahead of the partygoers and Odessa, with a salacious grin on his face.

Aimee planted her feet and swung at Trevor's face. "You deserve *this*," she declared triumphantly. "You mealymouthed prick."

Her knuckles connected with his chin, and his eyes rolled back. The impact of the punch toppled him over, and he fell backwards onto the onrushing partygoers, who all fell back down the stairs onto Odessa.

They went down in a heap like bowling pins at the base of the staircase.

The Pursuit

"Follow me," Aimee said as she turned back up the main staircase and ran toward the second-floor landing.

Rod and Darnell did as she said. As he ran, Rod glanced back at the scene forming at the base of the stairs.

Trevor, still dazed from Aimee's punch, was being held upright as he regained his wits. Odessa's face was twisted in furious rage as she clawed her way out of the mass of partygoers and climbed up on top of the heaving heap of people. She pointed her finger up the stairs.

"Get. Those. Fuckers. Now!" she screamed at the top of her lungs.

"Where are we going?" Darnell asked as they reached the second floor. He looked at the hallway across the landing from them, and the series of doors beyond Percy's office.

"We have to lose them somehow," Aimee said, looking up the stairs to the third floor as masses of partygoers started to swarm up both of the mirrored main staircases.

"Should we split up?" Rod asked.

"No!" Darnell and Aimee said in unison.

"We have to stick together," Aimee said.

Below them, behind the first wave of partygoers on the stairs, all of the people from outside were pushing their way in through the front door. The house was shaking from the stampede of angry faces storming toward the main stairs. The giant mob of enraged people flowed up the stairs led by a furious Odessa and a discombobulated Trevor.

"We've got to get to the third floor," Aimee said.

"What, are we going to jump off the roof?" Darnell asked.

"No! What? There's something up there that I need," Aimee said. "Or you could take your chances with them."

She gestured at the raving mob that was pursuing them. Darnell looked at the deranged crowd, and Rod looked right at Odessa's contorted, screaming face.

Rod looked at Darnell. "Yeah. We *should* go upstairs," Rod said.

"Okay, fine. Upstairs," Darnell said in a rush. "Let's hurry up."

Aimee sprinted to the third-floor stairs, and Rod and Darnell followed her.

The ravenous mob of partygoers continued to swirl up the stairway below them. Fortunately, most of the people in the crowd were in various states of intoxication, so they kept falling over, tripping each other up, and generally making slow progress.

Trevor's veins were pumping in his neck as he reached the second-floor landing before the rest of the people, then a wave of quicker partygoers spilled out behind him as Odessa followed.

The third floor was quieter than the two below. But the rumbling of the horde of enraged revelers shook light fixtures, tables, and windowpanes.

"This way," Aimee yelled, and they sprinted across the landing toward the western wing of the house.

A long hallway ran down to a large door.

"We have to find out what door this key is for," Aimee said, pulling the spindly silver key from the front of her dress and dangling it from its chain. Aimee started trying all the doors, one by one, in a rush.

"It's probably that one," Rod said, looking at the large, ornate door at the end of the hallway.

"Shut up, Rod," Aimee said, as she and Darnell kept opening doors.

They could hear Odessa and her horde spilling over onto the third-floor landing. The mob started to push into the narrow hallway, calling for their blood, still getting in each other's way.

"No, seriously, it's probably that one," Rod said in a nervous voice.

"Which one?" Aimee and Darnell snapped at the same time.

"Uh, the big one," Rod said, sprinting away from the encroaching mob. "With the fancy lock on it.

Right there! At the end of the hallway."

Aimee looked at the violent partygoers behind her, then looked at the enormous door and ran toward it. Darnell ran after them with the partygoers snapping at his heels.

Rod tried the handle to the door. It was locked.

The mob was closing in, snarling and howling as they clawed their way toward the three.

Aimee ran up behind Rod, inserted the key into the fancy silver lock, and turned the key.

The lock clicked open.

"I told you," said Rod.

Aimee gave him an exasperated look as she tried the handle.

This time, it turned.

The Library

Aimee, Darnell and Rod burst through the door and scrambled to lock and barricade it behind them. Breathing heavily from the sprint upstairs, they pushed a bulky, freestanding bookcase in front of the doorway. When they turned around, they found themselves in a dark, but comfortable private library. The ruckus of the crowd outside the door was muted here.

Electric light fixtures hung from the ceiling and walls, but when Aimee pressed the wall switch, everything remained dark. The room's only illumination was a faint light from its large floor-to-ceiling windows with heavy drapes that were held open with black velvet rope.

Tall bookshelves lined the walls. Pages ripped from books and papers covered in notes were scattered everywhere. There was a reading section over to the left of the room, chairs and tables and free standing ashtrays draped in shadow. To the right was a large marble altar. The workbenches were scattered with books, and tools lined the walls behind it.

Aimee caught her breath as she crept through the shadows to the windows. Rod and Darnell bumbled along behind her, still huffing and puffing. They could hear the chaos of the angry mob of partygoers battering at the door, but only faintly through the thick wood, as they looked down through the windows on the backyard. The grounds were still abuzz with activity below, as throngs of partygoers continued to flow into the house from around the grounds. The yellow-flame gaslights glimmered on the emptying lawn.

"What are we doing?" Rod asked, catching his breath. "We've blocked our only way out of this creepy room!"

"Yeah, Aimee, what *are* we doing?" Darnell asked. "I was supposed to take you to meet Percy."

"It's too late for that," Aimee said excitedly. "Don't worry, I have a plan. I think."

"What is it?" Darnell asked.

"Well, the first part was to use the key and find out what room it got us into. So that part was a success."

"And what's the second part?"

"I hadn't gotten that far," Aimee said as she walked cautiously over to the work area at the back of the room.

The heavy altar in the corner looked plain from a distance, but as she got closer, she saw it was covered in delicately ornate carvings. The embellishments created strange and intricate shapes in its surface.

Behind the altar by the bookcase near the wall was a large flag stand from which a heavy banner was hanging. It was a giant, dusty, old tapestry, with an expansive coat of arms showing a green shield floating on a field of red. The shield was separated into quadrants: the top left quadrant contained a pickaxe, the top right contained a sword, the bottom left quadrant showed a quill pen, and in the bottom right was a curiously twisted red curl.

"Open that door!" Odessa called. But her voice sounded muffled through the wall.

The door to the library was rattling in its frame, but it was holding firm.

Aimee walked up to the coat of arms and looked up at it with obvious surprise on her face. She looked back at Rod and Darnell.

"Guys," Aimee said. "This symbol looks familiar."

"What does it look like?" Darnell asked.

"It looks just like the Sequentia logo," she said quietly.

"Like the what?" Rod asked.

"Like where I work," Aimee said.

"See?" she said, pulling the case from her purse to show Darnell and Rod. "The logo on it looks just like this symbol."

"Oh, wow," Darnell said.

"But this tapestry has this curiously twisted shape, and mine has a rose in the bottom right," she said, tapping the ruggedized case with her index finger.

"What does it mean?" Rod asked.

"I'm not sure yet," Aimee replied.

"Well we'd better figure it out quick," Rod said as the mob of partygoers continued to batter away at the library door.

"Shut up, Rod," Aimee said. "I'm thinking!"

She began frantically inspecting all of the clutter on the work counter that ran along the wall. In the station in the very back corner, there was a large book on a stand.

It was a heavy, hidebound volume which had been placed under a magnifying glass mounted on an articulating arm. The tome was opened to a page depicting a curiously twisted shape.

"It's the same as the symbol on the shield," Aimee said in disbelief.

"How can these be here?" she asked. Her fingers were trembling, and her heart was pounding.

"Hey," Rod said. "I remember that shape."

"You do?" Aimee asked sharply. "From where?"

"From the roses," Rod said.

"From my dreams," Darnell said in a distant voice.

"And the knocker on the door," Rod blurted.

"Yeah!" Darnell agreed.

"What knocker?" Aimee asked urgently.

"That was the shape of the knocker on the door that led us here," Darnell said. "The one in the hedgerow."

"Are you serious?" Aimee asked. "This rune on this page is the same shape as the knocker on the doorway *I* came through!"

Darnell and Rod looked at her with their mouths

agape.

"This was on the door I summoned with my experiment," she said.

"What experiment?" Rod asked.

"Yeah, what experiment?" Darnell asked.

"The pages of this book look just like the parchment sample I studied," Aimee said, excitedly opening the small Sequentia Labs case, and pulling the folded, half page of parchment from it. "The one I used when I was building my machine. That I used to create the door."

She walked to the book and ran her fingers across the page with the rune while she felt the parchment in her hand.

She flipped to the very end of the book.

The last page of the book was missing, and when she unfolded her parchment and lined it up with the torn page, it fit perfectly against the edge.

Her head was swimming.

"What is this place?" she said.

"Aimee," Darnell said with concern. "What the hell is going on? We have to get out of here!"

The door was making a groaning noise under the weight of the partygoers.

"I don't know how long that door is going to last," Rod said tersely.

"I know! I just need a bit more time!" Aimee cried, frantically putting the parchment back in the case, and the case back in her purse.

On one of the bookshelves near the altar, amongst a pile of unkempt books, she found a row of pictures.

They depicted black robed figures gathered in groups. Sometimes they were standing around; other times, they were shown participating in orgies or performing arcane rituals. All of the pictures were in similar silver frames.

The last picture frame in the row was empty.

"This place is so fucked up," Aimee said, shaking her head.

"I knew you'd figure it out," Penny said.

Penny came out from where she had been slouched down low, watching them from one of the wingback chairs in the reading area.

"Oh shit," Rod said. "That creepy little girl scared the shit out of me!"

"Shut up, Rod," Aimee snapped. "Penny! How long have you been there?"

Penny ignored the question. "Come here," the girl said, motioning to Aimee.

They followed her to the bookcase, where Penny pulled out a box filled with photograph negatives and several prints. She pulled out a single glossy photograph.

"Look at this," Penny handed the photo to Aimee.

Darnell and Rod crowded around.

The black-and-white photo was marked with a handwritten date: October 13, 1923. Percy and Odessa were sitting in chairs facing the camera. Percy was slouched in the chair, his large frame slumping as if collapsing under its own weight. His eyes were sharp and bright behind his glasses, and there was a sheen of sweat covering his bald brow. Odessa sat straight-backed and imperious, her eyes cold and looking straight into the camera. Penny stood between them, wearing a tiny robe, not smiling. Percy had a hand on her shoulder, and Penny was leaning away from her parents with a sad frown on her face.

Behind the Gilbreths stood the rest of the group, all dressed in black robes, all with their hoods off.

Arthur Longfarthing was behind Percy, with his hand laid on the old doctor's shoulder, his wife Mary standing next to him. Trevor was behind Odessa, tall and darkly handsome, with the large book in his hand, a crooked smile on his pretty face, and his dark eyes twinkling malevolently. Fiona and Sinead stood next to him, running their hands over Trevor's shoulders. Klara stood farther to the right than anyone, a little space separating her from everyone else.

"What is this?" Aimee asked, her voice dropped to a nervous whisper.

"Listen," Penny said. "And I'll tell you."

Lucky Penny

A ring of eight, black-robed people chanted in a circle around Penny's tiny, hooded form. The little girl was laid out on the marble altar; Percy and Odessa, Arthur and Mary, Trevor, Klara, Fiona, and Sinead all chanted in unison around her. Their voices were muffled beneath the pointed hoods they wore over their faces, but their eyes glinted through slits in the fabric.

Poor Penny's head was covered with a thick black hood that had no holes for breathing or sight. Dark, red velvet was draped in thick piles over the altar, and spilled from beneath Penny's fragile form, flowing down the altar's sides in crimson waves.

Trevor led the group at the head of the circle, holding a large old book, as the chanting people performed their ritual in the private library. Their voices were muted by the rows of books lining the bookshelves that covered the walls up to the high ceiling.

A row of enormous floor-to-ceiling windows draped over with black velvet curtains lined the back wall of the room. Flames flickered in the candlesticks around the library, jumping fitfully with the rise of their voices.

The circle's menacing chanting increased in intensity, and a dark, otherworldly roar built slowly along with them. The deep roar escalated in a wave of sound and fury until it hurt the chanters' ears, and suddenly, Trevor snapped the ancient book shut with authority.

Everything became silent.

The dimly lit library was still.

The candles guttered in their stands, almost going out.

Through the old walls came the very slightest reverberation, the well-muffled sounds of the raging party down the hall. But they seemed distant. Inconsequential.

The ink-black shadows painting the room deepened, hinting at some vast unknowable thing that lurked beyond. A feeling floated in the air, barely tangible, like some inexorable force was being set in motion, some vast and ancient thing, reaching across from the beyond to touch this world.

The air was electric.

Trevor set the large book aside and slowly drew a long-bladed knife that gleamed in the light from the candles. Without a word, Odessa followed suit. After a slight hesitation Percy did too, then the rest of the circle pulled out their knives and raised them high.

The blades shimmered in the darkness. The low

roar returned, swelling and growing in volume and intensity.

The room—Penny's tiny form on the altar, the circle of hooded partygoers with their knives glowing in the dim light, the shadows enveloping them—it all took on a crystalline air. The roar grew until it whipped at their ears, and every molecule in the universe came into extreme focus for one split second.

Then they struck.

The blades all plunged at the same time, down into Penny, cutting through her skin and piercing her all at once, like some poor animal. The roar lifted into a formless, furious crescendo and ended abruptly with the last heartbeat of Penny's life.

A second passed.

The air was still. The rushing noise had stopped, but something remained: an ancient power. Though the world seemed like it'd just come to an end inside the confines of the old, thick walls, the circle of partygoers could once again dimly hear the murmur of the people outside the walls.

An uncomfortable moment passed.

Then Penny sat up abruptly.

Trevor and Odessa gasped, while Percy almost sobbed. Fiona and Sinead looked on with hunger in their eyes, as did Arthur and Mary Longfarthing, while Klara turned her head and looked away.

Penny's tiny body, still pierced by knives and bleeding into her thick black robes, silently pointed at something behind them all.

Slowly they followed her finger with their eyes.

On the wall, there was a door where no door had been. It was an old wooden thing with a curiously twisted iron knocker.

"It worked!" Trevor exclaimed.

"What do you mean 'It worked'?" Odessa asked suspiciously. "You said it would."

"Oh yes. Of course it worked. Yes, I knew it would," Trevor stammered.

"So what do we do?" Percy asked Odessa.

"Open the door," Penny commanded, interrupting.

Percy nodded and slowly tiptoed to the door. He stretched a tentative hand out toward it but paused.

"Do it!" Odessa hissed.

He complied and reached out to push the door. Before his hand could reach it, the door's iron hinges creaked as it swung inward slowly.

Wide-eyed, Percy peered into the inky blackness beyond. He couldn't see anything at first and squinted as he leaned in to see what secrets lay behind the door.

"What is that?" Percy asked.

A small spot lit up deep orange in the dark and flared bright with a crackle.

Percy stumbled back in astonishment.

David walked out of the doorway in a black, slim-fitting three-piece suit, wearing black leather shoes and a skinny black tie. His hair was dark brown and slicked back in an oily wave, and he looked at them all with dark eyes of some deep, indistinguishable color as he smoked a stubby unfiltered cigarette.

"Ah, oxygen is so gloriously … combustible," David said as he exhaled a cloud of smoke.

David walked over to Penny and delicately helped her start removing the knives.

"How are you feeling dear?" David asked her, attending to her gently.

"It hasn't been fun," Penny said in a rasping voice, blood bubbling on her lips.

"They really are unforgivable, aren't they?" David asked Penny. "I do hope you feel better soon." He smiled and patted her gently on the shoulder, setting the last knife down on the altar.

"So what about our immortality?" Trevor demanded.

"Yes! Never mind my spoiled daughter," Odessa said in acid tones. "What about our immortality?"

David turned to them and smiled. He inhaled from his cigarette and exhaled slowly before replying. "You'll get what you asked for," he said. "Though perhaps not in the form you thought."

"I don't care about all that. Just give me my fucking immortality," Odessa replied.

"And that was all they cared about, from beginning to end," Penny said as the door to the library bowed precariously, starting to splinter under the assault from the partygoers.

Penny turned and ran her small fingers along the altar, ignoring the chaos outside.

"They laid me right here," she said in a distant tone. "On this altar. On top of waves of red velvet.

And they killed me because they're selfish."

"All that for what?" Rod asked.

"To live forever?" Darnell followed up.

"Penny," Aimee said, aghast, "I'm so sorry."

All of a sudden, there was a loud bang, and the door to the library shifted in its frame. They all turned to look. The door was giving way. The mob was finally breaking through.

Broken Windows

A nother loud crash came from the breaking library door, startling Aimee, Rod, and Darnell. They looked away from Penny toward the ruckus coming from the entrance and then glanced back, but Penny was gone.

The door splintered, and Trevor pushed his arm and head through the shattered remains, glaring at Aimee. More arms sprouted from the hole as well, as they tried to push the bookshelf out of the way.

"I'm coming for you, Aimee!" Trevor yelled at them over the bedlam.

The door disintegrated under the force of the swarm, but the bookshelf still partially blocked the tide of furious partygoers. The incensed mass of people started trying to squeeze through the broken door, battering the teetering bookshelf.

However, before the throng of revelers finally broke through, Percy popped his head out of a dark nook in the bookcase near the reading area.

"Darnell, old bean. Is this the friend you told me about?" he asked, gesturing to Aimee.

"Yes!" Darnell said, and Percy nodded.

"You three have caused quite a commotion getting here," Percy said.

"Come on," Darnell said.

Rod made his way to Percy.

"But where did Penny go?" Aimee cried. "We can't leave her!"

The crowd swarmed over the bookcase.

"We *have* to go!" Darnell yelled as he grabbed her hand.

Rod began to run to Percy's stairway.

"Wait!" Aimee exclaimed.

"We can't!" Darnell said and pulled her toward Rod and Percy.

The bookshelf disintegrated beneath the partygoers as they flooded through the door. Odessa howled with rage, and Trevor smiled with delight as the mob cleared the path to Aimee, Darnell, and Rod.

"Aimee! Throw me the gun," Darnell cried.

"I can't. I lost it," Aimee replied in nervous haste.

"What!" Darnell burst out.

"Why would you do that?" Rod exclaimed simultaneously.

"I couldn't help it! Trevor attacked me!" Aimee cried.

"What!" Darnell and Rod both said in unison.

"For God's sake, quit bickering and let's go!" Percy said. "Odessa's in a fine temper today!"

Just as the wave of murderous partygoers was about to reach them, Raymond burst through the floor-to-ceiling windows, causing the black velvet drapes to billow inward in dramatic fashion as he swung in on a rope.

Odessa and Trevor and all of their malevolent followers looked up at Raymond's silhouette as he came feet first through the shattering windows. Glass rained down on the crowd in a glittering shower as he crashed through, barreling into Odessa and Trevor's army that crowded the library.

The nearest members went sprawling back into the people behind them, and in the shower of glass and midst of tumbling people, Odessa and Trevor were knocked down.

Raymond lunged for Odessa and Trevor, climbing over the heaving assemblage as he tried to get them.

"Run!" Raymond yelled over his shoulder at Aimee. "Get out of here!"

He glanced back at them one last time before the screaming man closest to him punched Raymond in the side of the face. A red-faced woman kicked him in the ribs with her high-heeled shoes.

"Go!" Raymond grated, pushing hard against the wall of people bearing down on him.

"Raymond!" Aimee cried.

"Go!" Raymond screamed as he was starting to be overrun by the partygoers as they surged back against him.

The last thing they saw was Raymond shoving a man back into the horde, causing the raging partygoers to all stumble backward once more, stopping the onslaught for a moment.

But only for a moment.

Then the partygoers were back on top of him, swinging, clubbing, and dragging him to the ground.

Percy ushered Aimee, Rod, and Darnell into the wall behind the bookshelves, then closed the door. They hurried up the narrow switchback staircase that was his passageway to the uppermost floor of the house, to his lab. They all followed him up the narrow stairs, heading toward whatever mysteries their future held in the dark reaches of the uppermost floor.

Rod's Fatal Mistake

Aimee, Rod, and Darnell followed Percy as he led them up the narrow staircase, Percy grasping the metal handrail to steady his heavy frame. They followed him toward the landing one floor up, while the door from the library below bent and shook from the partygoers trying to breach it.

"What about Penny?" Aimee asked.

"Don't worry about her. You'd be amazed how resilient children are," Percy said.

"I don't feel great about leaving her," Aimee said, her voice wavered.

"My dear, we don't have time for that. I hear you may have a mind for mechanical things," Percy said to Aimee, leading her along. "I want you to take a look at this infernal machine of mine."

"Do we have time for *that?*" Aimee asked in disbelief.

"We must make the time for this! It's of the utmost importance," Percy said as he led them up to the door at the top of the staircase. Once they reached the top floor landing, Percy slid open the small door to the lab and ushered them through. When he closed the door behind them, he pulled a lever that clanged a huge locking bolt across the door.

"That should buy us some time," Percy said.

"Whoa," Rod said as he entered the room and saw the shelves stocked full of preserved animal corpses that lined the entranceway. "What the hell are all these old animals doing in jars?"

"Come on," Darnell said, dragging him past the shelves and into the main lab. "Don't think about it."

Percy walked directly to the machine, and Aimee followed him, her eyes never moving from the giant device.

"I know this machine," she said, walking up to it.

"I see that," Percy said, smiling. "I can tell by the look in your eye."

"What the fuck is it?" Rod mouthed to Darnell.

Darnell just elbowed him.

"Shhh!" He said to Rod.

Aimee turned to Percy with a look of awe in her eyes.

"Who are you?" she asked him in a quiet voice. "You seem so familiar to me, like I've met you before."

"I am Dr. Percival Gilbreth of Sequential Experimental Laboratories, Incorporated."

Aimee's eyes widened in surprise. "Like, the founder of Sequentia Labs?" she asked in disbelief.

"But you disappeared almost a hundred years ago."

"Ah," Percy said. "Has it been that long? My poor brother. Artemis always did move slowly."

"What?" Aimee asked.

"Better late than never I suppose," he said.

"This machine," Aimee said, looking up at the hulking thing.

"May I show you how it works?" Percy asked.

"I know how it works," Aimee said. "It's just so old. It must be at least a Mark Three."

Percy watched her like a hawk.

"A Mark Three?" Percy asked. "My dear, this is my masterpiece, and I've named it for myself – the Percival Mark One. The very first and only one of its kind."

"This is the Mark One?" She asked him, finishing her inspection of it. "It's just like the early designs I studied." Aimee placed her hand on the machine. "I thought the prototype was destroyed in a fire."

"A fire? Apparently not," Percy responded. "This cursed thing has been up here in my lab, mocking me for an eternity as I've been trying to get it to work."

"But it won't, because it's missing something."

"Yes!" Percy agreed. "But we didn't have the facilities to make it here."

Aimee produced the Sequentia Labs case from her purse.

"Why does that little case have my family crest on it?"

Aimee didn't answer as she opened the case and pulled the delicate pink fuse from it.

"My God," Percy exclaimed "Is that what I think it is?"

"I made this back in my lab," she said. "And this is the very last one."

Percy looked at her dumbstruck as she inserted the last surviving fuse into the fist-sized hole in the front of the machine.

The old man's face lit up in wonder. "That *is* it!" He exclaimed. "That's the missing piece! The one that was too complex for me to make."

Aimee produced the piece of parchment from the Sequentia case.

"The plans you mailed to your brother. The plans he worked from to create the Mark Two after you disappeared," Aimee said, gesturing with the parchment. "The work that I completed with the Mark Ten."

She reached into the guts of the machine and adjusted some knobs and tensioners.

"Let me help you with that," Percy said, pulling back his cuffed sleeve and showing her the formula tattooed on his forearm.

She glanced at it for a moment.

"I don't need that," she said and reached into the machine. "Just turn on the power when I tell you."

Percy nodded and waited near the row of electrical switches on the wall behind the machine.

"Rod," Aimee said. "Get over here. I need you to pull that lever right when I tell you. Can you do that?"

Rod nodded and walked over to where Aimee was pointing at the machine.

As she was manipulating the buttons and dials,

she pointed over at another section of the machine where the gears and cams were packed closer together.

"Darnell," she said. "I need you over there. You have to make sure that knob holds steady while I'm setting up. And you have to turn it all the way up when I tell you. Okay?"

Darnell nodded, placing his fingers on the cold metal knob.

Aimee's fast-moving hands drastically changed the machine's settings.

"Don't you think those settings are too aggressive?" Percy asked.

"It's fine," Aimee said. "I know what I'm doing."

She turned and pushed the brass crank forward and down with a large kerchunk, priming the machine, whose finely manufactured pieces locked and interlocked as they moved forward a half rotation and clicked together.

"3 ... 2 ... 1," Aimee mouthed as she counted down.

She reached a count of zero and pointed to Percy. "Now," she said.

Percy flipped the series of smaller switches on the wall and then tripped the gigantic switch to connect the electrical circuit. The lights in the ceiling dimmed, and the readouts and dials on the electronic equipment lining the wall lit up with the surging electricity.

Aimee pushed the brass bar of the crank handle, quickly completing one full rotation of the mechanism. This final rotation ignited a flurry of activity in the bowels of the engine.

Arcs of electricity climbed between the metal rods of the machine.

The finely crafted parts of Percy's device moved faster and faster, their delicately machined movements hurried along by the constant stream of power. A high-pitched whine built up as the opulently engraved brass shapes spun, building momentum.

"This is faster than I've ever seen it work before," said Percy.

Aimee didn't respond to his concern. Instead, she looked at Darnell.

"Now, Darnell!" she yelled over the clangor, and Darnell turned the knob as far to the right as it would go.

The machine chugged and churned at a furious rate and began to emit larger and larger flashes of light as the arcs of electricity flowed between every part of it. The fuse itself began to glow violently with a shimmery rainbow aura that grew until the entirety of the room was lit up in overwhelming neon pink.

Aimee stepped back as the machine sped up and the amount of electricity it emitted grew more violent.

Underneath the clamorous sound of the machine, they heard a small, distant sound, like a whisper. At first it was quiet and seemed far away, but its volume kept growing in proportion to the ever-increasing speed of the machine's inner workings.

"Do it now, Rod!" Aimee yelled and stepped farther back.

Rod grasped the lever. Electric sparks ran through the bar and shot into his hands, but he hung on and pulled as hard as he could.

A giant flywheel in the center of the machine spun faster, gathering large amounts of energy, while the top of the machine started to light up.

"Now you two get the hell away from there!" Aimee yelled over the immense noise to Rod and Darnell as she backed further from the machine. Rod ducked away from the electricity arcing all around him, and Darnell dodged the bolts of power as well.

Darnell grabbed Rod's arm, and he tried to speak, but his words were drowned out by the machine and its enormous noise.

A giant lighting bolt shot from the top of the machine and connected to the ceiling. There was a huge sparking explosion, and the beam of electricity intensified, blowing the upper rafters and roof of the house away in a furious wave of power.

The starless sky above the house was now exposed through the remains of the charred and smoking rafters, and the beam of electricity grew in intensity as it reached up into the night.

The noise created by the infernal machine grew as it vibrated violently against its bindings. The roar became deafening, and the light from Aimee's filament became a blinding neon-pink flare. Aimee, Darnell, and Rod shielded their faces and turned from the maelstrom as it crescendoed.

Then there was a simple and clear popping noise.

The only other sound was that of the red-hot machine winding down.

The doorway appeared, heavy and wooden, with a

curiously twisted iron knocker.

The same moment the door appeared, so did David.

The mob of enraged partygoers finally managed to collapse Percy's locking mechanism, trampled through what remained of the laboratory door and its lock, and started spilling into the lab.

Odessa and Trevor rode the crest of a wave of red-eyed maniacs.

"Stop them from going through that door!" Odessa screamed, directing the mob toward Aimee, Darnell, and Rod.

Aimee ran as hard as she could toward it. Darnell and Rod followed her.

The snarling crowd of people led by Odessa and Trevor was so close behind their backs that Rod could feel the heat of their breath on his neck.

Aimee's fingers made contact with the door as members of the crowd grasped at Darnell and Rod, trying to drag them back.

Just as the wave of murderous chaos seemed like it was about to crash around them, David quietly raised a finger.

"Stop," he calmly said.

The horde of partygoers froze, kept in place by some unseen force.

David walked over to the machine, which was still slowing down, its glowing hot parts casting a red light on his face.

"What do you have to do with all of this?" Aimee asked as she turned away from the door to address

David.

"I only answered a summons," David said, the red light playing across his delicate features. "I just gave them what they wanted."

"That's all great but"—Darnell looked around at all the menacing partygoers frozen midrampage—"can we get the fuck out of here?"

He walked over to the doorway and opened it.

Nothing but blackness lay beyond.

Darnell took a step back.

"What is that?" He asked in trepidation.

"You'll have to find out for yourself," David said in a matter-of-fact tone. "Leaving is not the same as arriving."

While the two men were talking, Aimee had taken her cell phone from her black purse, and powered it on. The screen lit up, and she found she had a very small amount of reception.

"Yes!" she exclaimed under her breath. She fired off a quick text to her sister, pinpointing her location. The message went through on the meager signal.

"Guys, I'm not sure I want to go through this creepy ass door," Rod said, gesturing to the pitch blackness through the doorway.

David walked to Darnell, put his hand on his shoulder, and gestured at the blackness beyond the door.

"Do you want to stay?" he asked.

Darnell looked at the frozen looks of rancor on the faces of the angry partygoers that surrounded them.

"No, man, I don't," Darnell said.

"Well, you're going to have to go through that door to leave," David said. "It's the only real way in or out."

Rod walked up behind David.

"Then you go first," Rod said abruptly and pushed David through his own doorway. David pitched over and fell into the darkness, and the inky blackness swallowed him up.

"I got him!" Rod exclaimed.

The doorway cracked like lightning, then disappeared like a thunderbolt, leaving a spot of fractured light bending strangely where it had been.

The floor beneath them shook violently, warping immediately.

Cracks spread, swiftly spiderwebbing through the walls and ceilings of the house, and plaster rained down around them.

The whole house groaned and heaved as the ground quaked beneath it. Deep sounds of thick beams bending and breaking spread from within the house, and windows all along the exterior walls began to shatter in their panes.

The giant mob of partygoers that were all frozen midlunge became unfrozen and stumbled forward under their own remaining momentum.

Odessa and Trevor stared at each other in confusion.

Odessa, now unfrozen, gaped in horror as she stared at where the door once stood.

"Rod, no! You selfish asshole!" she howled pitifully.

"The doorway can't be gone!" Aimee said. "It was our only way out! We have to try again."

Odessa laughed, hollow and desolate.

"It's no use," she said bitterly.

"Shut up, woman," Percy said.

"But everything we worked for!" Odessa wailed.

"It wasn't worth it!" Percy spat. "If it ends tonight, so be it!"

"Shut up," Odessa shouted, as the walls and ground began to crack all around her.

"You both shut up!" Aimee yelled at them. "We have to start this machine again!"

"I don't think that's going to work," Darnell said.

"Why not?" Aimee asked.

Darnell pointed to the smoke billowing from the guts of the machine.

"It's on fire," Darnell said blithely.

Aimee ran over through the smoke to the machine and checked the filament.

It was a charred husk inside the glass housing. Smoke was pouring from the overheated apparatus as she reached into it, avoiding the flames to adjust some knobs.

"Aimee, we have to go," Darnell said.

"No!" Aimee said, continuing to fiddle with the machine. "This is our only way out!"

She cranked the handlebar to start the machine once more, and the entire enormous device erupted into a blue-and-red fireball, ejecting chunks of molten metal from the wreckage. Electricity arced out from the machine in crazed webs as flaming chunks set the room around them on fire, spattering the walls, the floor, the partygoers.

The crowd of people began stampeding away from the fire and arcing bolts of electricity, heading toward the exit to the room. Flames belched from the belly of the machine and burned up into the charred rafters with furious intensity, setting the room ablaze.

"Everything was going along fine before you ass-holes *doomed* us," Odessa said, staring at the flames as Trevor tried to drag her toward the stairs.

"So that's it?" Aimee asked in despair, her face lit by the spreading fire. "We're trapped."

"Dude, this sucks," Rod said, backing away from the flames.

"Well, don't complain too much. You did want to stay," Darnell said. "You got your wish."

They stared at the fiery wreckage of the machine, the hole in the ceiling above it, and the blood-orange flames consuming the walls surrounding it all, flames reflecting in their eyes. The waves of fire spread from the walls to the floor surrounding them.

The party was over.

It'd had quite a run.

End

Epilogue

Lunette drove up the Atlantic coast early in the morning. The sun shafted through the cover of leaves, and the trees soaked it up. Her car carved up the coastal road, with the Atlantic to her right and the great green canopy of Maine's woodlands to her left.

She sipped her Tiger Energy Drink and munched on a taco while steering her stylish little car around a left-hand corner.

She drove over a little bridge, and then she was on a tiny two-lane road which led into a comparably tiny town. An old iron sign on the side of the road read, "Welcome to Pfenigton." In town, there was a coffee shop, a tiny church, a run-down bar called the Randy Beaver, and a grimy little eatery called Pop's Diner.

She glanced down, looking at the map on her phone. A pin with a bright-red top sat in the middle of the screen.

"Aimee Xiao's Location," the pin's label read.

She passed through the little hamlet, and the road beyond the town curled away, like black ribbon strewn across the landscape. Little houses lined the side of the road, sporadically dotting the route to her sister's last known location.

"What the hell was she doing way out here?" Lunette asked no one aloud as she chewed the inside of her bottom lip.

She drove another twenty minutes or so until she passed the last old beach cabin on her right, which had trees drooping in the driveway and dark windows. She drove about half a mile further until she was adjacent to her sister's pin, which was a little off the road. She saw what looked like a faint, old, overgrown drive leading off the road. Her tires crunched on the gravel as she pulled onto the disused driveway and parked her car. She reached into the passenger seat and grabbed another taco from a paper bag of takeout.

Getting out, she walked into the woods and up the overgrown drive.

"Aimee? Aimee!" Lunette called her sister's name as loudly as she could.

The old path ended not far into the woods from the road, and there was no sign of anything resembling civilization from there.

She walked faster up the hill, to a little clearing on the top. She checked her phone, which indicated she was standing directly on top of Aimee's pin. Her hands were shaking as she continued to shout.

"Aimee!" her voice wavered. "Aimee?"

Her voice finally cracked, and she began crying.

"Aimee!" she cried, tears running down her face as she collapsed to her knees.

Then she was startled by a deep, authoritative voice: "Freeze."

Lunette gasped. She looked up and saw a man in unmarked black army fatigues pointing an assault rifle at her. Beside the armed guard, the pigmentless-eyed man, skeletal beneath his black wool trenchcoat, holstered his pistol. Another man in black military garb came up behind the first, pointing his assault rifle at her face.

Lunette dropped her taco as she put her hands up.

"Come with us," the first guard barked.

"Look what you made me do!" she cried.

The guards prodded their guns into Lunette's back as they marched her toward their van.

One of them opened the back doors to the van as the other told her, "Get in."

"Where's Aimee, you beast?" she asked the sharp-eyed man as she was loaded in. He got in the van behind her and sat in the seat directly across from her.

They looked at each other as he sat down: Lunette couldn't look away from the man's piercing, pigmentless eyes. They stayed like that for a moment: Lunette's heart rate increased, while the man said nothing.

They broke eye contact when the two rugged guards piled into the back with them and shut the heavy doors to the unmarked van.

The birds chirped in the trees as the van drove

away down the dirt drive, leaving the property, once again, undisturbed.

@

The Sequentia logo adorned the top of the glittering building of glass and steel. On the top floor, older men in finely tailored suits filed into the boardroom and took their seats around a long rectangular table.

Marky Steinbergen took his seat at the head of the table, his delicate mechanical frame whirred as he moved.

Behind him, there was a huge crest emblazoned on the wall, similar to a governmental seal – a green shield floating on a field of red. The face of the shield was separated into quadrants: the top left contained the image of a pickaxe, the top right a sword, the bottom left a quill pen, and the bottom right the rune.

A giant circle surrounded the whole image like a border. Across the top of the border, was the word "Sequentia." Across the bottom of the circle, emblazoned under the Gilbreth family crest in large ornate letters were the words, *"In aeternum vive."*

"How are we going to spin her disappearance?" asked one of the sweating board members.

"She'll be reported missing," someone said nervously.

"She already has been."

"Then all the more reason for us to move quickly and quietly."

The group of somber, well-dressed men all nodded

their heads in unison.

"We'll need to start a misinformation campaign."

"We can't take the blame for this. It would be disastrous for our stock price."

They all nodded again.

"Our agent already found someone snooping around the property. Turns out her sister reported her missing before we managed to detain her."

"Good," Marky said in an imperious tone. His frame whirred as he leaned forward, placing his elbows on the table, lacing his fingers together. "And find her sister. At any cost."

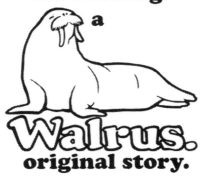

Thank you
for reading
a
Walrus.
original story.

Other great titles
from Walrus

STARS NEVER DIE

Cheated of her inheritance, Jessica Arkadin fights back against her twin brother Ansel in his quest to weaponize their late father's life changing mind-control technology.

DON' T BE AFRAID

by walrus

DON'T BE AFRAID

The world is moving too fast for Dylan Reynolds, and he's tired of being old and obsolete. He is willing to pay any cost to cheat death, but the future he's hoping for may not be what's in store.

Stay tuned for
more great fiction from

And remember, Walrus needs fish.

BTC

Made in the USA
Columbia, SC
06 March 2022

57026351R00164